"It's not a competition, Justin."

Another rueful smile. "Good thing." He sighed in something akin to defeat. "Because if it were, no question, you'd win."

And that bothered him, Amanda noted. Probably because he wanted to excel at everything he did. Silence and an aching awareness stretched between them. She felt compelled to remind him, "You know there are no perks that come with my presence here tonight or at any other time."

He nodded, accepting her boundary. For now, anyway. "How about we just be friends, then?"

Amanda scoffed. Now who was kidding themselves? "You and I can't be just friends," she said drily.

Another lift of his dark brow. "Why not?"

Amanda was sure he knew, but she decided to demonstrate the pitfalls anyway. She smiled and stepped closer. Keeping her gaze locked with his, she dared to say quietly, "I'll show you why not."

Dear Reader,

We all have goals and dreams. Some may even seem impossible. Until the day we realize we have no choice but to pursue them.

This is the case for Justin McCabe. He was the kid who did everything right—the kid with the great home and happy family, who had every opportunity.

Amanda Johnson had everything working against her: an unhappy home, little familial support, doors closed to her at every turn.

Growing up, both Amanda and Justin thought they knew what the future held. Then things changed. Justin saw a different, less privileged side of life. Amanda found family to love her and show her all that was possible.

Both ended up on a ranch for at-risk boys. The girl who'd been "nothing but trouble" and the "role model" of Laramie, Texas, shouldn't have anything in common. And yet...

I hope you enjoy reading this story as much as I enjoyed writing it!

For the latest news on these and other titles, please visit me on Facebook, Twitter and www.cathygillenthacker.com.

Best wishes,

Cathy Gillen Thacker

THE LONG, HOT
TEXAS SUMMER

———

CATHY GILLEN THACKER

HARLEQUIN® AMERICAN ROMANCE®

Recycling programs
for this product may
not exist in your area.

ISBN-13: 978-0-373-75465-6

THE LONG, HOT TEXAS SUMMER

Printed in U.S.A.

HARLEQUIN®
www.Harlequin.com

Chapter One

There were times for doing things yourself and times for not. This, Justin McCabe thought grimly, surveying the damage he had just inflicted on a brand-new utility cabinet and the drywall behind it, was definitely one of the latter.

Frustrated, because there was little he *couldn't* do well, Justin shook his head in disgust. Then he swore heatedly at the blunder that further derailed his tight schedule and made it even harder to prove the skeptics wrong.

It was possible, of course, that this could be fixed without buying a whole new cabinet. *If* he knew what he was doing. Which he clearly did not—a fact that the five beloved ranch mutts, sitting quietly and cautiously watching his every move, seemed to realize, too.

A motor sounded in the lane, and he hoped it was the carpenter who'd been scheduled to arrive that morning and had yet to actually make an appearance. Justin set his hammer down. He stalked to the door of Bunkhouse One just as a fancy red Silverado pickup truck stopped in front of the lodge. It had an elaborate silver Airstream trailer attached to the back and a lone woman at the wheel.

"Great." Justin sighed as all the dogs darted out the open door of the partially finished bunkhouse and raced, barking their heads off, toward the vehicle.

The obviously lost tourist eased the window down and

stuck her head out into the sweltering Texas heat. A straw hat with a sassy rolled brim was perched on her head. Sunglasses shaded her eyes. But there was no disguising her beautiful face and shapely bare arms. The young interloper was, without a doubt, the most exquisite female Justin had ever seen.

She smiled at the dogs, despite the fact that they were making a racket. "Hey, poochies," she said in a soft, melodic voice.

As entranced as he was, the dogs seemed more so. They'd stopped barking and had all sat down to stare at the stranger.

She opened her door and stepped out. All six feet of her.

Layered red and white tank tops showcased her nice, full breasts and slender waist. A short denim skirt clung to her hips and emphasized a pair of really fine legs.

She took off her hat and shook out a mane of butterscotch-blond hair that fell in soft waves past her shoulders. After tossing the hat on the seat behind her, she reached down to pet the dogs. The pack was thoroughly besotted.

Justin completely understood.

If there was such a thing as love at first sight—which he knew there wasn't—he'd have been a goner.

The woman straightened and removed her sunglasses. "I'm Amanda," she said in the same voice that had magically quieted his dogs.

Justin stared into long-lashed, wide-set amber eyes that were every bit as mesmerizing as the rest of her. His brain seemed to have stopped working altogether. His body, on the other hand, was at full alert. "I'm Justin McCabe."

"This the Lost Pines?" Amanda asked, taking a moment to scan their surroundings.

Working to get the blood back in his brain where it belonged, Justin merely nodded.

"So," she said, still admiring the acres of unfenced grassland peppered with cedar and live oak, as well as the endless blue horizon and rolling hills in the distance. "Where do you want me to park my trailer?"

And then, all of a sudden, the fantasy ended. This gorgeous woman had not been dropped into his life like a karmic reward for all his hard work. Brought swiftly back to reality, he stopped her with a regretful lift of his palm. "You can't."

She pivoted back to him in a drift of citrusy perfume. Her eyes sparked with indignation and her delicate but surprisingly capable-looking hands landed on her hips. "I made it very clear to whomever I spoke. My camping out here is part of the deal."

What deal? "It can't be."

She came closer, her soft lips pursed in an unhappy frown. "Why not?"

Embarrassed that it had taken him this long to correct her misconception, Justin explained without rancor. "Because this isn't the Lost Pines you're looking for."

A flicker of indecipherable emotion flashed in those beautiful eyes. She regarded him skeptically, seeming to think he was trying to pull something over on her. "But how can that be? The sign above the gate said this is the Lost Pines Ranch."

"The sign's on the long list of things waiting to be changed." A new one had been ordered but wasn't coming in for another month. Which meant he would continue to have these mix-ups with nonlocals.

"Are you sure I'm not in the right place?" she asked with a frown. "Because…"

Justin shook his head, a little disappointed that this beautiful amazon would not be settling in for a long stay. He turned and pointed in the opposite direction. "What you want is the Lost Pines *Campground,* which is another three miles down the road, next to the Lake Laramie State Park. But…" What the heck, why not? Just this once he was going to go for what he wanted. Which was a little more—make that a *lot* more—time with this sun-kissed beauty. "Once you get set up there, Amanda, I'd be happy to take you to dinner."

THIS WAS, AMANDA BLISS JOHNSON thought, the most bizarre encounter she'd ever had. Even if the tall rancher with the shaggy chestnut-brown hair and gorgeous blue eyes was the hottest guy she had ever come across in her life. From the massive shoulders and chest beneath that chambray shirt, to his long muscular legs, custom-boot-encased feet—and ringless left hand—everything about him broadcast Single and Available.

Which meant Strictly Off-Limits to her.

She wished she'd left her sunglasses on so he wouldn't see her dazzled expression. "First off," she told him crisply, "I don't date customers."

Now it was his turn to look shocked. "Customers! What are you talking about?"

Amanda pushed on. "You called for a carpenter, right? At least, Libby Lowell-McCabe, the CEO of the Lowell Foundation and chairwoman of the board for the Laramie Boys Ranch, did. She said it was an emergency. That your previous carpenter quit with no notice and you only have four weeks to get the bunkhouse ready for occupancy." She paused to draw a breath. "I emailed her back that I'd be willing to help y'all out, but only if I could keep my travel trailer on the property so I wouldn't have to waste time commuting back and forth to San Angelo."

Amanda fought her racing pulse and tried to stay calm. "But if that's not going to work, I guess I could park my

Silversteam at the campground. Assuming, of course, they have a space available. Since it's the busy summer season, they may not."

He lifted a hand. "You don't have to do that."

Amanda folded her arms in front of her. "Sure about that? Because just now you seemed dead set against me camping here."

He flashed a slow, disarming smile. "That's because I thought you were a tourist, not an apprentice."

Apprentice? Strike two for the handsome Texan! "I'm not the apprentice," Amanda said tightly, her temper rising. "I'm the master carpenter."

He pulled the paper out of his pocket and squinted at it as if he couldn't believe the words in front of him. Then his head lifted and he speared her with an incredulous gaze. *"You're A. B. Johnson Jr.?"*

Amanda wondered if it took him this long to process everything. "Amanda Bliss Johnson. Junior's the nickname I got at work."

"You want me to call you Junior?" he asked, with a hint of humor in his low baritone.

"Or Amanda." She waved a hand. "Whatever. It doesn't matter to me." What did was getting this gig. It would allow her to settle in this ruggedly beautiful place for an entire month before moving on to her next rural job.

Justin McCabe continued to contemplate her as if he either didn't believe she could really be an ace carpenter or wasn't going to be comfortable having a woman undertake such a large job.

Amanda sighed.

Great, just great. She'd gotten up at the crack of dawn to put the finishing touches on a built-in bookcase for a very fussy client, then spent hours getting all her stuff packed up and driving all the way out here. Now, the deceptively laid-back McCabe was acting like he wanted to fire her on the spot.

Deciding it was his turn to be put in the hot seat, Amanda stepped closer. "Do you have a problem with the fact I'm a woman?"

"No." He was clearly fibbing. "Not at all."

Then why couldn't he stop looking at her like he was going to need a protective force field just to be anywhere near her? "I come highly recommended." The defensive words were out before she could stop them.

"I know." He exhaled, beginning to look as off-kilter as she felt. "I just expected a guy. That's all."

A common mistake, given that most of her competitors were male. Still, Amanda refused to let Justin McCabe off the hook. Sensing there was more to whatever it was going on with him, she arched a brow.

There was a beat of complete and utter silence.

He scrubbed a hand across his face. "I did a Google search on your company after Libby told me she had arranged for A. B. Johnson Carpentry to come out and finish the work on an emergency basis. The website said the company was founded in San Angelo, Texas, by Angus 'Buddy' Johnson thirty-eight years ago."

Proudly, Amanda relayed, "That's my grandfather. He still runs the business—although he's supposed to be phasing out of that, too—but he stopped doing the rural gigs a year ago." After much persuading on her part.

Amanda touched her thumb to the center of her chest. "I do them now."

It was McCabe's turn to appear irritated. "So why didn't you make that clear in the communication with Libby? Unless—" he paused, still scrutinizing her closely "—you're trying to purposely mislead people?"

Amanda really did not want to get into this. However,

he'd left her no choice. "When I first started doing jobs on my own the company was getting a lot of requests for me that had nothing whatsoever to do with my talent as a carpenter."

Understanding dawned on his handsome face. Along with a hint of anger. Amanda warmed beneath the intensity in his eyes. "So we took all the employee photos off the website and just listed the carpenters by name, or in my case, just my initials and last name. To differentiate me from my granddad we added the Junior to my name. That successfully eliminated all the customers just interested in making up jobs to hit on me."

"Makes sense."

She straightened. "Luckily, that's not going to be the case here."

"No," he concurred, meeting her stern gaze. "It's not."

"Good to hear." Amanda relaxed in relief. The last thing she wanted to deal with was the amorous attention of the tall, sexy Texan. Given how physically attractive she found him, the situation might be just too tempting.

Thinking he was possibly the most easygoing man she had ever met, Amanda drew a deep breath. "Anyway, back to the way the company operates. My grandfather takes the service requests. He makes up the schedule and does all the accounting work required to run the business. The other four employees are all master carpenters, and they work in San Angelo. They all have families, and don't want to be away for days at a time, so I take the gigs on all the remote locations."

When he opened his mouth she lifted a staying hand. "Unless you're not comfortable with that? If that's the case, I'll see if one of the guys wants to do it." She paused again, frowning. "They'd have to commute back and forth, and the two hours' travel time daily would add significantly to the overall cost and time it will take to complete the job."

McCabe shook his head, swiftly vetoing that suggestion. "That won't be necessary," he reassured her. "You're here. You should do it."

Happy that much was settled, Amanda was ready to move on, too. She returned his easy smile. "Then how about you show me everything you want done so I can get started."

JUSTIN SPENT THE next half hour showing Amanda the bunkhouse they were converting for the opening of the Laramie Boys Ranch. It would house the first group of eight boys and two house parents. There were cabinets to install in the bathrooms. Trim and doors to put on. Bookshelves and built-in locker-style armoires to be constructed in each of the five bedrooms.

Amanda paused next to the mangled drywall and damaged utility cabinet in the mudroom. She brushed splinters of wood from the plumbing hookup for the washer. "What happened here?"

Motioning for the dogs to stay back, well out of harm's way, Justin grabbed a trash bag. "I tried to put the cabinet up myself and it fell off the wall, taking the drywall with it."

Amanda dropped the shards of splintered wood and ripped-up drywall into the bag. Justin knelt to help her gather debris.

"Can you fix it?" He wasn't used to screwing up. Failing in front of a highly competent woman made it even worse.

"Yes." Amanda dusted off her hands and took out her measuring tape.

Justin watched as she set down her notebook and measured the damaged back of the cupboard. "No need to order a new cabinet?"

Nodding, she jotted down a set of numbers.

When she had finished looking around, Justin asked, "What's your best estimate?"

Amanda raked her teeth across her lush lower lip as she consulted the list she had made. "You said you wanted hardwood flooring installed throughout?"

"Except for the bathrooms. Those are going to have ceramic tile."

"The target date?"

"August first."

"Which gives us a little under four weeks." She tilted her head slightly to one side, her hair brushing the curve of her shoulder. "That's an ambitious schedule."

"Is it doable?"

"That all depends. Are you willing to have me work weekends and some evenings, too?"

Until more donations or grants came in, things were really tight. "We don't have the budget for overtime pay," he admitted.

Understanding lit her eyes. "I'll just charge you the regular rate, then."

He paused, tempted to accept yet not wanting to take advantage. "Sure?"

She tucked her notebook under her arm and headed for the open front door. She stepped outside, the sunshine illuminating her shapely legs. "Consider it my donation for your cause. Which, by the way, is a good one."

Justin fell into step beside her as they continued toward her truck. "You think so?"

She tossed him an admiring glance. "Troubled kids need a place to go." A hint of a smile curved her lips. "If that can happen in a beautiful setting like this, more power to you."

"Thanks." Not everyone was on board with his idea for the ranch. It helped to know she was.

The dogs raced forward, suddenly on full alert. A split second later, a car motor purred in the distance. Two vehicles appeared, the second one a black-and-white Laramie County sheriff's car.

"Another lost tourist?" Amanda joked, her glance roving over him once again. "This one with a police escort?"

Justin shook his head, hoping it wasn't more bad news. "Mitzy Martin. She's the social worker tapped to work with the ranch. She's also on the board of directors. The sheriff's deputy is my brother Colt McCabe. He's in charge of community outreach for the department. I have no idea who the teenage boy with her is...."

Amanda backed up. "Well, obviously you don't need me for whatever this is." Giving the other visitors a cursory wave, she walked to the truck, his dogs trailing behind her, and began unloading her tools.

The teenage boy stayed put as Mitzy and Colt got out of their cars. Both radiated concern as they approached. "We have a favor to ask," Mitzy told him.

Justin looked at the sullen teen slouched in the passenger seat of Mitzy's car, arms crossed militantly in front of him. Pale and thin, he wore a black T-shirt with a skull on the front. His dark ash-blond hair was on the long side. "What's up?"

Mitzy shot him an imploring look. "We need a place for Lamar Atkins to stay during the day for the rest of the summer."

Understandable, but... "The ranch isn't open yet."

Colt inclined his head toward the unfinished bunkhouse. "It looks like you could use a lot of help getting it ready."

That much was certainly true, particularly in the bunkhouse. Justin paused, wanting to make sure he knew what they were expecting him to provide. "You want me to pay him?"

Mitzy shook her head. "Help him work off his community service hours."

"For…?" Justin prompted.

His brother frowned. "Repeated truancy. He's supposed to be in summer school now, but he keeps skipping, and the judge gave him one hour of community service for every hour of class he's skipped. Which amounts to two hundred and thirty-six hours."

Justin muttered a compassionate oath. That was going to take a while to work off.

"If you take Lamar on, and he sticks with the program, he'll be finished with his community service commitment before school starts in the fall," Mitzy urged. "And hopefully will learn something in the process."

Justin looked at the kid. He had his earphones in, his eyes closed. Justin turned back to Mitzy and Colt. Both had also felt the call to help others. Although his brother was now happily married and father to a little boy, Mitzy was as single as Justin was, with as little time for her social life as he. All three of them took to heart the fate of those in need. "Where are the boy's parents?"

Mitzy's expression tightened. "Long gone. Fed up with trying to deal with his defiance, they severed their parental rights and turned him over to the state last March. The court placed him with a foster family in Laramie, but both foster parents work during the day, and they can't be around to constantly monitor Lamar." She paused. "He seems to like them, and they feel the same way about him, but they just can't keep him in summer school."

Justin squinted. "What happens if this doesn't work out?"

"Given that Lamar was already on his last chance when

I picked him up?" Colt exhaled slowly. "He'll be labeled incorrigible and put in a juvenile detention center."

Which meant an awful lot was at stake. Justin had seen enough kids spiral downward. He didn't want to be personally responsible for the ill-fated future of another. "I want to help." Wanted to give the kid a safe place to be during the day.

Mitzy regarded him with confidence. "We figured you would."

"But…" Justin cast a glance over at Amanda, who was lifting toolboxes and a power saw out of the bed of her truck. "I'd feel a lot better about it if the place was finished and the live-in counselors were here."

"You still want to be named ranch director by the board?" Colt asked. "Instead of just chief financial officer?"

Justin sighed, frustration growing. "You both know I do."

Mitzy pushed, sage as ever. "This is your chance to prove yourself worthy of the job."

Justin knew Mitzy and Colt were right. This was a prime opportunity to advance his career in the direction he wanted it to go, as well as a chance to help a kid in need. So the situation wasn't perfect. They'd manage. "When do you want to start?"

The duo smiled their thanks. "First thing tomorrow morning," Mitzy said.

"So you're going to personally supervise Lamar?" Amanda asked in shock after Justin filled her in an hour later.

To his aggravation, she seemed to think he couldn't— shouldn't—do it. "Why does that surprise you?" Justin was more than a little irked to find her among the naysayers who were constantly doubting him.

Amanda surveyed the area surrounding her temporary home site. "From the way you were talking earlier as you showed me around, I had the impression you were more of a numbers guy."

Being good at something didn't mean it was the right fit, career-wise. Justin wished he could make people understand that. He followed her back to the trailer. "I studied business and accounting in college."

Amanda chocked the tires so the trailer wouldn't roll. Finished, she stood. "What practical experience have you had working with troubled kids?"

Not enough; he'd found out the hard way. But that, too, was about to change.

"I worked at a nonprofit that helped at-risk teens." He helped her unhitch the trailer.

Amanda undid the safety chains. "And did what exactly?"

"Initially, I was the CFO." Justin pitched in and took care of the sway bars. "Eventually, I coordinated services for the kids, too."

"But someone else did the actual counseling and evaluating," Amanda guessed.

Justin nodded. "Which was quite extensive, given how complicated some of their situations were."

Her expression pensive, Amanda unlocked the hitch. "I'm sure it was."

"But?"

Amanda got into her truck to drive it out from under the hitch. "Facilitating services for an at-risk kid is not the same as actually getting through to him or her." She stepped back out of the cab and headed toward him, her long legs eating up the expanse of yard.

Unfortunately, this wasn't the first time Justin had heard

that particular argument. "I can do this." He knew it in his gut. All he needed was a chance.

She gave him a skeptical look, then took out a carpenter's level to check the floor of the trailer. As she moved, the hem of her denim skirt slid up her thighs. "From what you've just told me, Lamar sounds like a tough case." Finding it okay, she stood with a smile. "Forgive me for saying so, but you don't seem like someone who knows much about defying the system."

Justin couldn't deny that was true. He'd gone through life without getting into trouble with authority once. That didn't mean he couldn't help those who had.

He was beginning to feel a little irked. "So?"

"Where's the common ground that will allow you and Lamar to establish any kind of rapport?"

"He'll respond to time and attention."

Amanda shook her head. "You think his foster parents haven't been giving him that?"

"Obviously, Lamar needs even more than what he's been getting," Justin countered. "Which is where I come in."

Amanda activated the trailer's solar panels. "Want my advice?"

"No, but I expect you're going to give it anyway."

Their eyes met. "Leave the life lessons to the social workers. They've had lots of practice and they're good at it."

She went inside the trailer and returned with a rolled-up awning, which he helped her set up.

"Work on getting this ranch finished and ready for the first eight boys. If Lamar can help you do that, fine, it'll be a good deal for both of you." With the awning finally attached, she brushed dust off her hands. "But accept the possibility that the kid might not want to be here tomorrow any more than he apparently wanted to be here today."

"And if that happens?" he prompted, intrigued despite himself by her perspective on the situation.

Her voice dropped a companionable notch. "If he doesn't want to help out, don't force it, because the only way it will ever work is if this is his choice. Not someone else's."

Justin studied her closely. "What makes you such an expert on all this?" *As compared to, say—me?*

A hint of sadness haunted her eyes. "Because I lived it. For a good part of my teenage years I hated everyone and everything."

Now, that was hard to imagine. She seemed so content and comfortable with herself. Sensing he could learn something from her, Justin asked, "What changed?"

For a moment, Amanda went very still, seeming a million miles away. "Me. I finally realized I had a choice to either continue on as I was, which was a pretty miserable existence, or approach life differently. The point is, Justin, you can't help someone who doesn't want to help himself." She sighed. "From what I saw, it didn't look to me like Lamar is there yet."

He grimaced at the truth of her words. "I know he's not."

Another beat of silence. "Then?" she pressed.

I'm not risking another tragedy. It's as simple and complicated as that.

Justin stepped closer, vowing, "I'm going to help Lamar whether he wants me to or not." He paused to take her in, appreciating both her beauty and her strength. "I'd like it if you were on board with that. If you're not," he paused and shot her a laser-sharp look, "I'd appreciate it if you would keep your feelings to yourself."

Chapter Two

"I'd rather work with her." Lamar pointed at Amanda, soon after arriving the following day.

Justin motioned Lamar back to the stacks of paper he had been trying to organize. Some were for state licensing and registration, others were for federal, state and private grants. The biggest—a quarter-million-dollar endowment from the Lone Star United Foundation—was due by the end of July. In addition to that, there were more fund-raising solicitations to send, thank-you letters to write, a tight budget to manage and local building regulations to comply with.

Justin had figured the teen would show up with an attitude, but he wasn't going to let him dictate how things were done. "Not an option."

Lamar slouched in his chair, a scowl on his young face. "How come?"

"Because Amanda's not in charge of you," he reminded the boy mildly. "I am."

The teen returned his glance to the window. "That wood she's carrying looks heavy."

Heavy enough to require the sleek muscles of her gorgeous shoulders and upper arms, Justin noticed appreciatively. What it did for her legs wasn't bad, either.

Justin dragged his glance away from the statuesque

beauty in the sleeveless red T-shirt, denim coverall shorts and sturdy work boots. "If Amanda needed our help, she would've asked for it."

"Sure about that? I mean, isn't this place supposed to be about turning kids into well-mannered guys? What kind of Texas gentleman lets a lady hoist all that stuff by herself—even if she is a carpenter by trade?"

Good question. And one meant to make Justin bend to Lamar's strategy. "Nice try."

The kid held his palms aloft. "Hey! I'm just saying…"

Justin eyed the paperwork still needing attention. "Did you get how to use the scanner? Or do I need to explain it again?"

Lamar turned back to the desk with a huff. "I'm not good at this computer stuff."

Which was an understatement and a half, Justin soon found out. In the next thirty minutes, Lamar managed to accidentally shut down the operating system, re-enter a single document three times and delete two files Justin had initially scanned as examples. The only thing worse than his own mounting frustration was the fact that his young charge seemed equally annoyed at his own ineptitude.

"So maybe office work isn't your thing," Justin said finally, ready to admit that all this assignment had done so far was cost both of them precious time and patience.

Lamar looked wistfully out the window at the vast blue horizon and dazzling sunshine. "Sure you don't want me to go out and at least offer to give Miss Amanda a hand? She still has quite a bit to unload."

The goal was to get Lamar doing something constructive on his very first day, so Mitzy could report back to her superiors that things were going well.

Figuring it would be okay if they both assisted Amanda, Justin stood. "All right. Let's go ask."

Justin and Lamar walked out of the lodge. By the time they reached the pickup truck that Amanda had parked just in front of the door, she had re-emerged from the bunk-house. She looked from one to the other. Sweat beaded her face, neck and chest. "What's up?" she asked, blotting the moisture on her forehead with one gloved hand.

Justin turned his attention away from the pretty color in her cheeks and the radiant depths of her eyes. "We thought we'd give you a hand with the unloading," he explained.

Amanda stiffened. "That's okay. I've got it."

Lamar gave the pretty carpenter a pleading look. "If you don't let me help, he's going to make me go back to the computer—and I've already messed things up in there pretty bad."

Amanda had no problem turning Justin down.

Lamar, it seemed, was another matter entirely.

She sized up the teenager. "The bunkhouse air-conditioning isn't installed yet. My guess is, even with all the doors and windows open for maximum airflow, it's about a hundred degrees inside. Add physical exertion to that, and it's going to be a workout and a half," she warned.

The tall, lanky teen was evidently unconcerned with the hard physical labor ahead of him, so long as he got out of any more office work. "Okay with me," Lamar said cheerfully.

Justin smiled and offered, "I can help, too."

Amanda frowned. "That's okay…you don't have to. Lamar and I can handle it."

Justin didn't like feeling expendable.

But if this was what it took to get Lamar to realize he could actually enjoy being out here on the ranch, Justin figured he could spare him for one day. "Let me know when Lamar's work for you is finished," he told Amanda briskly. "I'll take it from there."

AMANDA KNEW SHE had hurt Justin's feelings. There was no helping it. She could not have him underfoot. He was too handsome, too distracting, and she couldn't afford to lose her focus for even a moment.

"You know, if you don't want me around, either, I could go off somewhere and just get lost for a while," Lamar suggested casually as soon as Justin had gone back into the lodge.

Chuckling, Amanda clapped a gloved hand on his shoulder. "Nice try, kid. But you told Justin you'd help carry all this wood into the bunkhouse, so that is exactly what you're going to do." She rummaged around in her truck and returned with a pair of leather work gloves for him.

Awkwardly, Lamar inched them on. "You don't mind taking orders from him?"

Did she? Normally, Amanda liked to maintain her independence and set her own work agenda. That was what made these rural gigs so appealing. The clients were so busy with their own work, they were less inclined to micromanage her. Best of all, at the end of the day, she could really get away from it all in her home-away-from-home travel trailer.

"Justin McCabe runs this ranch. It's my job to make sure he is happy with the work I do. Yours, too, for that matter, since he's overseeing your community service."

Silence fell.

Lamar stacked more trim wood in the corner, next to a pile of interior doors that needed to be installed. "Don't you want to know what I did to get sent out here?"

Amanda brought in a stack of doorknobs and latch kits. "Truancy, right?"

Lamar scowled. "Justin told you."

They walked back outside for another load. "Yep."

Lamar peered at her from beneath his blond bangs.

"Aren't you going to use this opportunity to lecture me on how I'm ruining my life and all that?"

Amanda took in the front of his Pirates of the Caribbean T-shirt. It depicted a rollicking fight scene. "Would you listen?"

"No."

She handed him a bundle of trim wood. "That's what I figured."

Lamar cradled it against his chest. "Which is why you're not lecturing me."

Amanda grabbed a bundle for herself and walked with him toward the door. "I figure there has to be a reason you keep cutting class."

Lamar put down his bundle of wood with more than necessary force. "I hate it. It's boring."

Regular school had been a pain for Amanda, too. Figuring they could both use a rest, she went to the cooler in the corner and brought out two icy grape-flavored electrolyte drinks. She tossed one to him. "What does interest you?" she asked.

Lamar wiped the moisture away with the hem of his shirt. "I like watching TV. Listening to music."

Amanda took a long drink. There had to be something that would help him connect with others. "Do you play any sports?" Even if Lamar didn't qualify for school teams, there were always private athletic leagues to provide a little fun and make him feel involved.

"Nah." Lamar finished half his bottle in a single gulp. "I'm no good at sports, either."

So Lamar had suffered multiple failures, socially and otherwise. Catching sight of his dejected expression, Amanda's heart went out to him. She knew was it was like to be a teenager who didn't seem to fit in anywhere. "What *are* you good at?"

Abruptly, mischief crept into his expression. "Getting out of stuff I don't want to do."

Amanda could see that. "You can't really make a living as a no-show."

"So maybe I'll be a security guard," Lamar boasted, "and sit around and watch those TV monitors."

Amanda couldn't think of anything less interesting, but leery of discouraging him, she smiled. "Could work."

He paced to the window and back. "You're not going to try to talk me out of it? Tell me I have to finish high school and go on to college?"

Amanda held his gaze. "College isn't for everyone."

"Did you go to college?"

Amanda shook her head. "I didn't like high school, either, so I got a GED instead and learned carpentry from my grandfather."

His face grew pinched. "I don't know about the GED," he grumbled, as if it were the worst idea in the world. "All that studying and having to take those tests…"

Amanda could see where even the idea of that would be overwhelming for Lamar, given he'd skipped so much he had to be way behind on his studies. They walked back out to the truck to finish unloading supplies.

"Do you like being a carpenter?" Lamar asked eventually.

"Very much."

He slanted her a wary glance. "How come?"

Trying not to think about the failures in her own life, Amanda offered him a faint smile. "Because I like building things that will last."

It was nearly noon when Justin looked up from behind his desk to see his dad striding into the lodge. As he walked across the spacious living area, Wade McCabe held a large high-velocity floor fan in each hand.

Justin strolled out of the administrator's office to greet him. "Hey, Dad. Thanks for bringing those out." Wade set them down next to the overstuffed sofas and chairs that had been donated by a local furniture store. "Some reason you couldn't run into town and pick them up yourself?"

A very good one, as a matter of fact. "I'm supervising a teenager's community service right now."

His dad looked around, perplexed, noting they were quite alone.

"Lamar's in the bunkhouse, assisting the carpenter. He'll be back in here as soon as they're finished carrying in all the wood from the pickup truck."

His dad paused. "So this is a one-day thing?"

"All summer."

Wade blinked in surprise. "You're not really equipped for that, are you son?"

Justin tensed. *Here we go again.* He turned and walked into his office. "Dad, if this is where you tell me if I'm serious about all this, I need to go back to school and get a degree in psychology…"

Wade looked around the sparsely decorated administrator's office, which at the moment was littered with the paperwork Justin was still trying to get through. "Your mother and I raised you to find what you're good at and do it to the best of your ability." He sank into a chair in front of Justin's desk and gave him a long, level look. "What you are good at, Justin, is finance and accounting."

Justin slid a stack of papers into a mailing envelope, sealed it shut and ran it through the postage meter. "I'm doing that here."

Wade steepled his hands in front of him. "To a much lesser degree than what you were doing five years ago."

Which, for his ambitious father and mother, was unacceptable, Justin knew. They wanted all five of their sons to have the same kind of financial security and success they'd built for themselves, while still holding on to their core values. "It's important work, Dad."

Wade's expression softened. "I'm not discounting that. It's why I made a sizable donation to help get the Laramie Boys Ranch up and running and accepted a position on the board of directors."

Something Justin was beginning to regret. In hindsight, he saw answering to his father, even among a group of other involved adults, might not be such a good thing. "Then...?"

"Your mother and I are worried about you."

Justin grimaced. "Why?"

"Clearly, you've yet to get over everything that happened in Fort Worth—first your broken engagement to Pilar, and then..."

Justin heard a feminine throat clear, followed by a knock. He and his father turned to see Amanda standing in the open door.

"I'm sorry to interrupt," she said, looking gorgeous as ever, despite her hot and sweaty state. "But have either of you seen Lamar?"

ACTUALLY, GIVEN THE conversation she'd overhead inside the ranch's office, Amanda wasn't at all sorry to interrupt. It sounded as though Justin McCabe needed a break. Having been the target of a great deal of parental lecturing growing up, she knew just how demoralizing such sessions could be. Not to mention the damage they inevitably did to the relationship. Although, unlike her mom and dad—who had seen her mostly as a stumbling block to their happiness—Justin's parent seemed to genuinely care about him.

She continued, "I just got back with more wood and…"

Justin shot out of his chair, his expression filled with concern. "What do you mean you *just got back?*"

Why was he making a big deal out of this? "I had to run to the lumberyard to pick up the rest of the baseboard." She paused. "He didn't tell you?"

Justin shoved a hand through his hair. "I haven't seen him. I thought he was with you."

Justin's father looked on with a mixture of resignation and disapproval.

Amanda felt for Justin. Whether or not the two of them should have seen this coming was a moot point. She swallowed uncomfortably. "He should have reported back to you about an hour and a half ago…."

Justin stalked around the desk to her side. "Where could he be?"

Amanda turned to let Justin through. She caught a whiff of soap and man as he passed by. "I don't know." She was, however, willing to help search.

Together, the three of them looked through the lodge. Eventually, they found Lamar sound asleep in the lounge on the second floor. The TV was on, the sound turned all the way down.

Relieved yet still disapproving, Wade McCabe told his son curtly, "I'll leave you to handle this."

Tense with embarrassment, Justin nodded at his dad. "Thanks again for bringing the fans."

Wade nodded and left.

Lamar opened his eyes, stretching lazily. He smelled of sweat and bubblegum. "Hey," he said to Amanda. "You're back."

"Yes." She tried not to think about how much trouble Lamar was already in, and he'd only been at the ranch for half a day. "I am."

Justin clenched his jaw with frustration. "Is this where you've been the entire time she was gone?" he demanded.

"Yeah. So?"

"You were supposed to find me when Amanda no longer needed your help."

Lamar rubbed the sleep from his eyes. "Yeah, well, all you were doing was office work. I'm no good at that."

Justin gave Lamar a reproving frown. "That's not for you to decide. This is community service, remember? To get credit for your time, you have to do what you're told."

Lamar sat up and dropped his feet to the floor. Belligerence radiated from him in waves. "Is it time for lunch yet?" he asked, completely ignoring Justin's reprimand. "I'm really hungry."

Amanda's stomach had been growling for the past half hour, too. "I've got some sandwiches made if anyone wants to join me."

"Sounds good to me," the teen said.

Amanda looked at Justin. Temper again under control, he nodded. Then he cautioned Lamar, "Just don't do that again, okay? For both our sakes, I need to know where you are at all times."

"Okay," Lamar muttered.

Relieved to have that settled, Amanda led the way to her trailer. She invited the guys inside, figuring there was safety in numbers. Wrong. The moment they stepped inside, her refuge felt filled to the brim with testosterone. And much smaller. Especially with Justin standing right beside her. Of course, that was probably because at six foot five his head almost reached the ceiling.

"Wow!" Lamar whistled appreciatively as he surveyed the comfortable space she had worked so hard to create. More a mini-apartment than camper, the back half was all bedroom and bath. The front half of the Airrstream housed the kitchen—with a full-size fridge, microwave, stove, sink and even a tiny dishwasher. The butcher-block tabletop between the roomy banquettes doubled as a work space, and there were plenty of built-in racks for her pantry items and cookware.

"You must really like to cook." Lamar checked out the bins of fresh fruits and veggies, her complex variety of dried chili peppers and some freshly made tortillas.

Amanda nodded proudly. "It's a hobby of mine."

"Where did you learn?" the teen asked.

She opened up the fridge and brought out the three large grilled-chicken wraps with lettuce, cheese and Caesar dressing that she'd made from the leftovers of the previous evening's dinner. "My grandmother and grandfather. Cooking was something they liked to do together, so when I moved in with them I started cooking, too."

"Sounds fun," Justin said.

"It was." It was the first time she'd known what it was like to be part of a happy family.

The handsome Texan's fingers brushed hers as she handed him a flavored sports drink. "Was? You don't do it anymore?"

Trying not to react to the husky caress of his voice, the warm feel of his fingers or the tenderness in Justin's brilliant blue eyes, Amanda shook her head. "Occasionally, but not as much since my grandmother died of congestive heart failure a couple of years ago."

"Sorry to hear that," Justin and Lamar said in unison.

Amanda accepted their condolences with a nod, aware of a growing sense of intimacy she didn't expect. Wasn't supposed to want. And knew would be unwise to encourage. "So," she said, pushing her lingering grief away. "Why don't the two of you tell me a little more about the area. What should I know about Laramie County?"

"There are a number of good restaurants in town," Justin began.

Lamar nodded. "The Lone Star's food is good, and they have live music and dancing, too. Since chicks seem to like that stuff," the teen added helpfully.

Amanda wondered if that was where Justin had intended to take her the first night, when he'd asked her out.

"I do like dancing," she admitted with a smile.

Justin's eyes gleamed. "Then you should make it a point to go while you're here," he said. "With or without a date."

Amanda's middle fluttered with sensation. Adopting her best poker face, she nodded. "I'll keep that in mind."

Wary of letting her thoughts wander where Justin's were obviously headed—into forbidden romantic territory— Amanda guided the conversation to mundane subjects, like the new wind farm and a famous sculptor she'd heard about who worked in bronze.

As soon as the meal was over, she rose. Eager to get back to work, she looked at Justin. "Your dad said he brought two fans that would help cool off the bunkhouse till the air-conditioning is installed?"

Justin nodded. "Lamar and I will carry them over for you."

Amanda smiled. "Great. I'll meet you guys there."

A few minutes later they walked in, and Amanda showed them where she wanted the fans set up. Concerned that there was still a lot of friction between Justin and Lamar, she figured it wouldn't hurt to act as buffer a little while longer.

"I don't know what you had planned for Lamar this afternoon," she told Justin, "but my work will go a lot faster if I have assistance mounting the top kitchen cabinets."

"I'll do it!" Lamar quickly volunteered.

Justin looked at the cabinet lift Amanda had set up, and

the bulky stock cabinets. She knew he could see it was not an unreasonable request, even if she could easily have done the job all on her own. "Can you keep him busy the rest of the afternoon?"

"I won't let him out of my sight," Amanda promised.

Justin exhaled, his expression grim. After a long pause, he gazed at Lamar. "No more disappearing acts. Okay?"

The teen nodded, clearly aware he was on very shaky ground with the man supervising his community service.

Justin turned back to Amanda, his eyes devoid of the gratitude she had expected. "I'll be in the office, working on grant applications, if you need me." Justin turned on his heel and stalked off.

Watching him go, Amanda knew she had just made another mistake. She should never have stepped between Justin and his charge. In the end, all she had done was make things worse.

As soon as Justin disappeared from view, she did her best to undo the damage. "You need to give Justin a chance."

His expression stony, Lamar helped her cut a base cabinet out of its cardboard cover. "McCabe doesn't get me the way you do."

Amanda bit her lip. "I'm not so sure about that." While it was true that she could talk to Lamar with ease, Justin seemed to have Lamar's number in a lot of ways.

The boy's jaw tightened. "I see the judgment in his eyes when I screw up, Amanda. I don't need any more of that."

She had seen the disappointment, too. However, it didn't mean Lamar had to return it in kind. "You're going to have to work with Justin while I'm around, and after I leave. So the sooner you try to find common ground with him, the better."

Lamar picked up the utility scissors. "Maybe I could

continue my community service with you, wherever you go after this," he suggested hopefully.

Amanda was flattered. She also knew it wasn't the best idea. She cut open the next box. "I don't think the court is going to go for that. They're going to want to see that you can follow the rules and act in a positive manner, no matter where you are or who you're with."

Lamar sulked but said nothing more.

Her point made, Amanda focused on the cabinet installation. She kept Lamar busy until his foster father showed up to collect him at the end of the day.

Only when she'd had a chance to get a shower and clean up a little did she go in search of Justin again.

She found him on the back deck of the lodge with his dogs.

"Got a minute?" she asked, aware she owed him an apology, but unsure if he'd accept it.

Justin measured kibble into five stainless-steel bowls. He had the same brooding look he'd worn when he'd been talking with his father. "It's probably not the best time for us to talk, Amanda."

Not an encouraging start. "We need to clear the air."

After each dog had a bowl of food he turned to her. "Go ahead."

She swallowed. "I'm sorry if I got in the way of whatever you were trying to accomplish with Lamar this afternoon. But I thought a time-out between the two of you might help. And I used the opportunity to tell him he should give you a chance."

His gaze drifted over her before returning ever so deliberately to her eyes. "Bet that went over well."

Like a lead balloon. "He'll come around." Amanda punctuated her words with a hopeful look.

He stood, legs braced apart, arms crossed in front of him. "Is that all?"

She wished. "I have a feeling you blame me for Lamar skipping out on us this morning."

"I'm sure he would have done the same thing whether you were here or not."

She lifted her chin. "Then why are you ticked off at me?"

Leaving the dogs on the patio, he turned and strode back into the lodge. "I'm not."

"And if I believe that, you've got a lake in Odessa you'd like to sell me."

Justin walked down the hall to his office where stacks of paper and letters littered every available surface. Frustration emanated from him in waves as he took a seat behind his desk. "Let's just say it wasn't the best day for me, okay?"

Amanda refused to give him sympathy. He was throwing enough of a pity party all on his own.

"I don't deny there were issues," she countered. "But to be honest, the problems were also of your own making. I mean, really," she continued, goading him with thinly veiled exasperation, "could you have given Lamar a worse task on his first day here?"

Justin's glance narrowed. "What do you mean?"

Not about to let him pull rank on her—because in this instance they were equals—she moved around the front of the desk and leaned against it, facing him. "Lamar was sent here because he can't stand school. So the first thing you do is give him *paperwork*?"

His full attention on her, Justin rocked back in his swivel chair and waited for her to go on.

Her frustration with the situation boiling over, Amanda

continued, "Does anyone know why he is skipping so much? Has anyone even asked him?"

Justin's handsome features sharpened with chagrin. "I don't know what he's told others, but I can tell you that I haven't discussed it with him."

Hands cupping the edge of the desk, her arms braced on either side of her, Amanda leaned close enough to search his eyes. "Don't you think you should?" she persisted.

Justin's brooding expression returned. "I'm not his counselor."

Amanda exhaled and sat back. She knew this wasn't her problem, and yet it was. "Then try being his friend."

His jaw hardened. "He's got to respect me first."

Amanda knew better than anyone that a solely disciplinarian approach never worked with a kid like Lamar, just as it had never worked with her when she was ticked off at the entire world. "Set a good example. Inundate him with kindness and patience. The respect will come."

Silence fell between them. She couldn't tell what Justin was feeling. Wasn't sure she wanted to know.

Restless, Amanda stood and began to pace around the room. She paused to look at some of the awards hanging on the wall. There were several for community service and fund-raising, as well as his bachelor's degree diploma from the University of Texas. Also on display were a model and numerous sketches of the Laramie Boys Ranch as it would look when it was completed with a dozen residential bunkhouses, barns and corrals, basketball and tennis courts, and a swimming pool. But the walls were devoid of the kind of pictures that one would expect to see—portraits of family and friends, and kids he had helped in the past. Truth be told, there was nothing uniquely personal here.

Wondering if his quarters at the ranch were any different, she swiveled back around. "I know your heart is in the right place," she said softly, determined to help him succeed with Lamar.

He raked his hands through his shaggy hair and stood. "You just don't think I'm cut out for this."

Amanda paused, her hands curving over the back of an armchair. It was difficult telling someone what they didn't want to hear. For whatever reason, with Justin, it was ever harder. She met his eyes. "Kids like Lamar are complicated. They're tough to reach because they play everything so close to the vest."

His broad shoulders relaxing slightly, Justin roamed closer. She inhaled the brisk masculine scent of his skin and hair, her pulse picking up another notch.

"So how did you get through to him?"

Feeling as if the room was a little too warm and small for comfort, Amanda turned and walked into the spacious living area with its abundant couches. She sank into a big armchair, wishing she could find the right words to reassure him. "I didn't. Not really." Pretending she wasn't oh-so-aware of every masculine inch of him, she looked Justin in the eye, then lamented, "All I can tell you for certain is that Lamar's self-esteem is incredibly low."

Justin rubbed the underside of his handsome jaw. "Which is why he's acting out."

Trying not to notice how good it felt to be with Justin in such an intimate setting, Amanda fought back a flush. "Right."

Justin sat on the sofa opposite her. "Still." Justin paused to look her over lazily, head to toe. "You connected with him a lot more than I did. He followed you around like a lost puppy."

Tingling everywhere Justin's gaze had touched, and everywhere it hadn't, Amanda shrugged. She knew that what she and Lamar had shared had, for the most part, been superficial, that there was much more going on with the teenager than he was divulging. There had to be, given the fact Lamar had been abandoned by his parents before becoming a ward of the state.

Aware Justin was still studying her intently, Amanda slanted Justin a haphazard glance. "Lamar had never actually seen any carpentry work being done, so he was interested in what I was doing."

"Plus," Justin guessed ruefully, "Lamar was trying to get out of more desk work, assigned by yours truly."

"Good point." A more companionable silence fell, and they exchanged smiles. "I want this to work out for you both," she said.

Really listening now, Justin leaned forward a bit. "Then where would you suggest I start?"

Amanda tried to keep her eyes off the sinewy lines of his shoulders and chest. She did not need to be wondering how it would feel to be held against him. And she certainly didn't need to be wondering what it would be like to kiss him!

Amanda smiled and advised, "By doing something with Lamar tomorrow that would get you both out from behind a desk. Something that needs doing that he can feel good about at the end of the day."

Justin took her advice to heart. "I'll work on it," he promised, leaning toward her. "In the meantime, I have a favor to ask."

Chapter Three

"A favor," Amanda repeated, wondering why she was so drawn to him. And even more important, why she was so curious. He was just a client. She shouldn't need to understand Justin McCabe on a personal level, never mind try to figure out why he had taken on a challenge of this nature. And yet, she sensed there was *something* motivating him. Something he didn't like to talk about.

"Don't worry." Justin rose and headed for the lodge kitchen. "It's nothing all that drastic."

Intrigued, Amanda followed him. "I can't wait to hear it, then."

Justin wandered over to the fridge and peered inside. He took out a package of New Braunfels smoked sausage links and set them on the counter. "I volunteered to host a fundraising dinner and I've got no clue what I need to do to get ready for it…or even what kind of food I should serve."

Amanda couldn't have been more shocked had he proposed marriage. "And you're asking *me?* The carpenter?"

Justin set a skillet on the stove. He opened a bottle of Shiner Boch beer and poured it into the skillet, then added the links and turned the burner on to simmer. "You're still a woman. And you like to cook." He went back to the fridge and brought out containers of pre-made German potato salad and green beans with almonds. "I figured you would know this stuff."

Amanda did. Unfortunately, she had gone down this particular path before, and it wasn't a mistake she intended to repeat. "Isn't this the kind of thing you should be discussing with your girlfriend?" she asked.

Justin went to the fridge again and brought out two more bottles of beer and a jar of jalapeño barbecue sauce. "Don't have one." He opened both beers and handed her one.

Their fingers brushed, sending a thrill spiraling through her. Amanda took a small sip of the delicious golden brew and studied him over the rim. "Don't have one as in you recently broke up with someone, or don't have one as in you don't want to be in a relationship?" she asked before she could stop herself.

The corner of his mouth quirked up and he took a drink. "You really want to know?"

"I do," she murmured. *Though maybe she shouldn't*...

He let out a long breath, then turned and dumped the green beans into a saucepan to heat. "A couple of years out of college, I got engaged to a woman I worked with." The words seemed to come with difficulty. "Pilar and I were both vying for promotion. But there was only one slot available at the company where we worked, and the competition for it was intense. I'd been there longer, had an edge. So Pilar picked my brain at length about what I thought it would take to land the top job, then passed my ideas off as her own before I could present them to my boss." He took another sip of beer. "Suffice it to say, she got the promotion."

"That's terrible!" Amanda blurted out, stunned by the depth of his ex's betrayal.

"The worst of it was that Pilar didn't think she had done anything wrong." There was a long pause as Justin lounged against the counter. "She said that the corporate world was brutally competitive and to succeed one had to be ruthless. She was only surprised I hadn't done the same to her, or at least tried. But—" cynicism crept into his low tone "—she felt we could still go on, forewarned and forearmed."

Amanda couldn't believe her ears. "Obviously, you felt otherwise."

"I realized I didn't want to be in a relationship where competitiveness was a factor. So I ended it."

"Over her objections," Amanda guessed.

"Yes."

Amanda couldn't blame him for brooding. Setting the bottle aside, she closed the distance between them and squeezed his hand compassionately. "I would have done the same thing in your place," she admitted.

"What about you?" He drained the remainder of his beer. "Is there a reason you don't want to help me out? A boyfriend waiting in the wings who might not approve?"

Hoping Justin hadn't picked up on how attracted she was to him, because an awareness like that could propel them right into the bedroom, Amanda flushed. She moved a slight distance away and worked to contain the emotion in her voice. "I'm not attached, either. Although, like you, I was engaged once, several years ago."

His gaze scanned her face and body, lingering thoughtfully, before returning to her eyes. "What happened?"

"Rob's parents got wind of the fact that I had a less-than-admirable record before I went to live with my grandparents."

His gentle expression encouraged her to go on. Amanda drew a bolstering breath. "They heard from one of their friends, who managed a department store, that I had been caught shoplifting there. As you can imagine, my potential in-laws were not pleased. They had in mind a very different type of woman as the mother of their grandchildren."

He caught her hand when she would have turned away. "So your fiancé broke up with you?"

Amanda leaned into his touch despite herself. "I broke up with him. I didn't want to come between Rob and his family, and I certainly didn't want to have kids with a man whose own parents detested me."

Justin turned around and brought out two plates. "And Rob didn't try to persuade you otherwise?"

Noting that Justin had simply assumed she'd dine with him, Amanda shook her head. "In the end, he agreed a long-standing family quarrel wasn't what he wanted, either."

"And since then…?" Justin asked, seeming to understand implicitly how devastated the whole debacle had left her.

She decided she might as well eat with him—she was starving and he had enough food to feed four people. "I've had dates here and there, but nothing with the potential to be lasting."

It seemed the kind of guys she wanted to date all had stellar childhoods and stable, loving families. In the end, none wanted to be dating a former delinquent.

The most vulnerable part of her did not want to find out that Justin felt the same way.

Justin loaded their plates with food and motioned for her to sit down at the stainless-steel work island that ran down the center of the room. He took a seat and his smile turned seductive. "So there's really no reason you shouldn't help me, then."

Except that it would bring them closer, and she wasn't sure she wanted to be closer to someone who made her feel this wildly excited and yearning for more.

She liked the way she had been before. Content with what she had, and who she was. Not longing for the Cinderella fantasy of a spellbinding romance.

Aware Justin was still waiting for her answer, Amanda settled onto a high-backed stool opposite him. "Don't you have a mother or a sister or someone else you could ask?" Her mouth and throat had suddenly gone bone-dry.

He added a healthy splash of barbecue sauce to his plate and cut into his sausages with gusto. "I don't have any sisters. My four brothers know as little about party planning as I do."

"There's still your mother," Amanda persisted.

Justin set the barbecue sauce in front of her. "She's a wildcatter, with her own company to run. Not only is she completely inept in the kitchen—to the point that it's a running family joke—she's pretty busy scoping out a new drilling site in the Trans-Pecos area of southwest Texas."

"So," Amanda said, picking up her knife and fork, "it's back to me."

Laugh lines crinkled at the corners of his eyes. "That lunch you served us proves you're an amazing cook."

She kept her eyes locked with his, even as her heart raced in her chest. She took a bite of the meal he had prepared. The sausage was delicious—crispy on the outside, meaty and flavorful on the inside. "This is really tasty, too."

"The supermarket deli made half of it."

Amanda felt her face flush even as she savored the tang of the German-style potato salad. "One excellent home-cooked meal is not going to get you what you want."

"Sure?" His eyes danced with merriment. "Because there are more meals where this came from."

Amanda raked her teeth across her lower lip. She knew he was attracted to her, too. Sparks arced between them every time they were near. "Is this just an excuse to spend time with me?" she asked warily.

He dabbed at the corners of his mouth with his napkin, poker-faced once again. "I said I wouldn't hit on you while you were working here."

And he hadn't. The problem was, she was beginning to want to proposition *him*. At least in fantasy…

Heat climbed from her chest to her neck and face. "I believe that you really do need help for this worthwhile cause, but why does it have to come from me? Surely you could hire a party planner or caterer."

Finished eating, Justin leaned toward her, forearms on the table. "We don't have the budget for that. Plus, word would get out. And since entertaining is going to be part of the ranch director's job…" He let the thought trail off.

Unbidden, another wall came tumbling down. One that, perhaps, should have stayed intact. "So to help them take you seriously, this has to be well-done," Amanda guessed.

His mesmerizing blue eyes found hers. "You got it."

She bit her lip, intrigued despite herself. "How many guests are you going to have?" She did like cooking for a crowd.

"Twelve," he replied, setting his glass down. "Thirteen, if you'll come and speak to the rest of the guests about your own experiences turning your life around and how it led to you becoming the upstanding adult you are today." He glanced at her admiringly. "Because clearly whatever it is—whatever it takes to connect with an at-risk kid—you have in spades. I can see it in your dealings with Lamar and the way he instinctively relates to you."

Amanda didn't know what was worse. The thought of wanting to hit on Justin—when he was so obviously off-limits and out of her league. Or being simultaneously recruited to plan and cook for his party *and* be the star of his dog-and-pony show on dysfunctional childhoods.

Thoroughly insulted, Amanda set down her napkin and stood. "I have to hand it to you, McCabe. You really know how to make a gal feel good."

He seemed taken aback by her sarcastic tone.

"The answer is no," she snapped. "To all of the above."

And no to the idea of ever making a play for him, as well. Heaven help her, she thought wearily as she strode from the kitchen. *When would she ever learn?*

THE NEXT MORNING, it didn't take Lamar long to notice the atmosphere. "Is Amanda mad at you?"

She'd certainly taken his compliments—and request for help—the wrong way, Justin admitted ruefully.

Wishing he had even a small part of Amanda's natural ability to communicate with troubled kids, Justin asked his teenage charge, "Why would you think that?"

"I don't know. I saw her shoot you this look when she was heading over to the bunkhouse. She was definitely angry."

Justin sighed and ushered Lamar through the lodge onto the back deck, where the sun was already beating down. The heat had risen past an uncomfortable ninety-five degrees, and it was barely past nine o'clock. "I may have ticked her off last night when I asked her to do me a favor that would help out the ranch." Justin whistled and all five dogs came running.

Lamar hunkered down to pet them and was soon covered with doggie licks and kisses. Reveling in the unchecked affection, Lamar looked up at Justin. "That doesn't sound like Amanda. Seems like usually she's happy to help out with stuff. She even volunteers. Like with lunch yesterday. I mean, she didn't have to feed us, but she did."

"Yeah." Justin had also been surprised by this morning's standoffish attitude. "Maybe I just caught her at a bad time."

The only thing he knew for sure was that Amanda had felt used or manipulated. Which rankled. All he had really wanted was to find a way to bring down the barriers she had erected around herself and get to know her better. So something else a heck of a lot more satisfying than just friendship might be possible. But that hadn't happened. Worse, he had undermined whatever small gains he had made in his pursuit of her.

And he was, Justin admitted reluctantly to himself, pursuing her. Despite the fact he had promised not to make a pass at her. While she was working on the ranch, anyway. Once that was done, all bets were off....

"Am I going to be helping her today?" Lamar asked hopefully as he gave the dogs a final pat and rose to his feet.

Justin pushed aside the disappointment that he was still a less than acceptable choice from the teen's point of view. But, like Amanda said, he had to remedy that by giving the kid something he could accomplish and feel good about. "No, you're going to be assisting me," Justin said, ignoring Lamar's immediate scowl of displeasure. "First off, we need to give the dogs a bath."

Dismay quickly turned to trepidation. "All five of them?"

Justin nodded, figuring the task would take a good part of the morning to accomplish. "They need to be bathed before we put on their monthly flea and tick medicine."

Lamar shoved a hand through his hair. "I don't know if I'm going to be any good at that, either."

Justin refused to let fear of failure get in the way, for either of them. "Do you know how to pet a dog?"

"Sure…"

Justin smiled and pressed on, "Do you know how to take a bath yourself?"

The boy scoffed. "Well, duh."

"Then you've got all the skills you need." Justin went into the mudroom off the kitchen and pointed to the shelves. "Grab the leashes, that stack of towels and the box of treats." Justin picked up the rest of the supplies and stepped out onto the long deck that ran along the back of the lodge where the dogs were still waiting curiously.

One by one, Justin roped the leashes to the railing and then snapped the secured leashes to their collars. He asked Lamar to turn the water on and bring the hose up on the deck. Already sweating himself, Justin adjusted the hand-held sprayer to the shower setting and handed it over to Lamar. "Let's wet them all down first."

While he did that, which also cooled the dogs off, Justin made sure the towels were well out of the way and opened up the shampoo and conditioner bottles. He handed one of each to Lamar, instructing, "Soap, rinse, condition and rinse again."

The teen nodded, looking both serious and nervous, but Justin knew the kid would do fine once he actually got started. "Why don't you start with Sleepy, since she's the most patient?"

Lamar knelt down next to the dachshund–bassett hound mix. Sleepy lay on her side, lazy as ever and ready for a nap. Already starting to panic, Lamar looked at Justin. "How am I going to wash her?"

"Start with what you can reach." Justin drizzled a line of shampoo down Roamer's spine and began working it into his soaked coat. "She'll get up."

Lamar looked over at Justin and mimicked his actions. The teenager frowned at the dog's fur. "It's not lathering."

"Did you use shampoo? Or conditioner?" Justin asked,

belatedly figuring out what had happened. It was an easy mistake to make—the white plastic bottles all looked the same. Only the labels were different.

"Oh. Conditioner, I guess."

"It's okay. Just rinse it out and pour on some shampoo."

Lamar seemed frazzled. It didn't help matters when Woof, who was still waiting his turn, began to bark hysterically.

"It's okay, Woof," Justin said firmly. "Calm down."

Reacting to the excited hound, Fetcher strained at her leash then took it between her teeth. Justin knew it wouldn't take much to chew through it and reprimanded the Labrador–golden retriever mix. "Fetcher, drop!"

Assuming they were involved in a tug-of-war, Fetcher pulled all the harder on the woven fabric lead. Anxiously, Woof intensified his barking and howling. Professor—the poodle–black Lab mix who hated chaos of any kind—began to look for a way out. Any way out.

"Fetcher! Stop!" Justin warned, reaching past Roamer to comfort Professor.

Meanwhile, apparently hating the feel of the shampoo on his back, Roamer rolled around on the deck, trying unsuccessfully to rub the soap out of his coat.

Realizing it would have been better to hook up two hoses, Justin waited while Lamar rinsed the foam off Sleepy.

Justin handed the teenager the appropriate bottle with one hand; with the other he worked to pry the leash out of Fetcher's teeth. "Condition next," he instructed.

Lamar frowned, perplexed. "I already did. Before I shampooed, remember?"

Justin grimaced as Fetcher clamped down harder on the leash and tugged with all her might. Meanwhile, Woof continued making a racket.

Justin had to shout to be heard over the growing commotion. "Condition *after* you shampoo!"

Professor, deciding he'd had enough of the ruckus, began yanking against his leash, using all his weight to pull free. Justin leaped to put a stop to that. Which was, as it turned out, all the opportunity Roamer needed. One jerk of the German shepherd–border collie's long elegant neck and he was out of his collar. Still covered with swirls of shampoo, Roamer left the dangling leash and collar behind, bounded over the backs of Woof and Sleepy and raced across the long veranda just as an unsuspecting Amanda rounded the corner.

ONE MOMENT, AMANDA was on her way to see what all the hubbub was about. The next, eighty-five pounds of wet black dog rammed her legs. The impact knocked her off her feet and sent her sprawling so hard onto the wooden floor of the deck that the wind was knocked from her lungs. Roamer splayed awkwardly over her, equally stunned by the collision. He whimpered and licked her face as if to make sure she was all right. Dimly, Amanda was aware the barking and howling had stopped. She blinked again and saw Justin hovering over her, his handsome face taut with concern. Then she noticed Lamar, who was apparently just as worried.

"Amanda!" Justin physically removed his still-confused dog who sat, suddenly compliant. "Are you okay?" he asked, kneeling down beside her.

Feeling a little better, but never comfortable as a damsel in distress, Amanda started to rise. Justin slid an arm around her waist and helped her into a sitting position. "I'm fine." She looked over at the half-bathed dogs, realizing why there had been so much commotion. She made a face. "You were bathing the dogs all at once?"

"It's what I usually do," Justin admitted defensively.

Lamar edged away, shoulders slumped, mouth tight. "Except this time I screwed it up."

Knowing the last thing the youth needed was another setback, Amanda shook her head and answered in the same tone her grandfather used when she needed bolstering, "No, you didn't. No one did." She paused to give the skeptical teen a long, level look. Then she smiled, letting both guys know she really was okay. "Dogs just get excited sometimes."

His hands still cupping her shoulders, Justin shot her an appreciative look that warmed her almost as much as his tender, protective touch.

"Do you have a dog?" Lamar asked, coming closer.

Amanda let Justin help her all the way to her feet. Realizing belatedly how soggy her T-shirt was, she plucked it away from her chest. She smelled like wet dog—as did the guys. "No. I always wanted one, though."

Lamar leaned down to pet the now-quiet circle of animals. He regarded her curiously, and the sense of near-familial intimacy between the three of them deepened. "Why didn't you get one, then?"

Amanda was aware that Justin was listening intently. "None of the adults in my life wanted to take responsibility, so I knew if I got a pet, I'd be completely on my own. I guess I was worried I'd let him or her down."

"You wouldn't do that," Lamar protested.

It was good to know someone thought so. Unfortunately, Amanda knew better than anyone that she was better at short-term relationships, in general, than anything requiring a lifetime commitment. Only with her grandparents had she been able to forge something lasting. And that hadn't happened until they had taken her in and put her on solid footing.

Lamar turned to Justin, not above pleading, "Maybe Amanda should help us finish giving the dogs a bath. Then we could do her a favor by helping her with the carpentry."

Amanda didn't want to cut into Justin's time with Lamar. However, she *did* want to boost the teen's confidence. And, given the mess the two guys had made of the doggie baths, it was clear they needed help getting back on track. "Okay."

Justin blinked in shock at her quick acquiescence, which probably surprised him given the irate way she had walked out on him the evening before.

A little embarrassed that she had been so emotional last night—she could have just said no and left it at that— Amanda continued matter-of-factly, "I've got some heavy lifting that needs to be done, and I was headed over here anyway to see if I could borrow you both for an hour or so. Now I won't have to feel bad about asking since I'll be helping you fellas out first."

"We would have helped you anyway," Justin countered, in a way that let her know he was thinking about her curt refusal to *his* request for aid the night before.

Amanda refused to feel guilty about that. It had been a bad idea. It was still a bad idea.

She squared her shoulders and lifted her chin. "Yes, but this way we'll be even."

Lamar squinted at them. "Am I missing something?"

"No," Justin and Amanda said in unison, despite the chemistry sizzling between them.

Again, Lamar took note.

Wanting to move on, Amanda took a deep breath and asked Justin, "So which dog do you want me to bathe?"

Justin paused. "Probably better take Woof. Fetcher's still pretty rowdy."

No kidding, Amanda thought, watching her recommence rolling around on the deck as if wrestling an invisible opponent, her leash once again clamped in her teeth.

"I'll finish Roamer and then start on Fetcher," Justin continued, getting back down to work. "Whoever finishes first can handle Professor."

"So how long have you had your dogs?" Amanda inquired, picking up a bottle of shampoo.

"I adopted Sleepy and Woof when I was still living in Fort Worth and working at a nonprofit there. They came from a shelter. Professor and Fetcher came from families here in Laramie who thought they could handle having a pet and then discovered they couldn't." His voice thickened with emotion. "I found Roamer on the side of the road. He was painfully thin and infested with fleas and ticks. It looked like he had been driven out to the middle of nowhere, abandoned and forced to survive on his own."

Amanda's eyes filled just thinking about it. "That's awful."

Lamar's jaw clenched in youthful indignation. "How can people do that?" he asked fiercely. "When you adopt a dog—"

Or have a kid like Lamar, Amanda thought.

"—it's supposed to be a lifelong commitment!"

Only sometimes it wasn't, Amanda thought sadly. "I guess some people aren't cut out for that kind of responsibility." She waited for her turn with the hose, then wet Woof down and lathered shampoo into his fur.

Lamar became even more irate. "Well, you can count my parents in that tally," he muttered.

Deciding the only thing that would comfort Lamar was total honesty, Amanda confided, "And mine."

Lamar's jaw dropped. "You got ditched by your folks, too?"

Beside Amanda, Justin went very still. She realized

these were the kinds of intimate details that Justin had wanted her to share with his dinner guests—to help them understand the plight of an abandoned child, from the child's perspective—and she had declined.

Having shared it once with a man she trusted, and suffered the fallout, she wanted to keep the miserable story to herself.

Yet, realizing it might make Lamar feel less alone to hear her story, Amanda forced herself to continue. "My parents divorced when I was two. I spent the next twelve years bouncing back and forth between their houses." She sighed heavily. "Both remarried and divorced, more than once, so to say it was chaotic is an understatement. I wasn't happy about it, and I showed my displeasure by acting out."

Lamar finished bathing Sleepy before turning his attention to the patiently waiting Professor. "How?"

Amanda shook her head in regret. "I skipped school. Shoplifted. Raided the liquor cabinet of a friend's parents'. Threw parties. Secretly sneaked out to movies I wasn't old enough to see." Out of the corner of her eye, she could see Justin listening intently.

"Wow." Lamar sounded impressed.

Amanda held up a cautioning hand. "It's not as glamorous as it sounds, Lamar. I came really close to ending up in juvie. Luckily, before that happened, I tried to run away. The local police found me and took me to the station, where I officially entered the system, and a sympathetic social worker decided I needed more stability than either of my parents were able or willing to give. She talked my grandparents into taking me in."

Amanda paused, remembering. "They had rules. Lots of them. I had to study for my GED and be respectful, help my grandmother around the house and work as Granddad's apprentice when I had any spare time."

Lamar reached for a bottle, paused, as if unable to decipher the labels. "And that was a good thing."

Noticing he needed the conditioner, Amanda handed it over, and was rewarded with a grateful smile. "Yep. For the first time in my life, I really felt safe. And loved. And cared for." She paused to towel off Woof, taking care to dry his face and ears before his body, just as she had seen Justin do.

That accomplished, she continued her story. "The point is, even though my parents couldn't handle me or my problems, I eventually ended up in a better place. I was happy." She paused to let her words sink in and saw Justin was a captive audience, too.

She turned away from Justin's tender expression. Swallowing, she pushed on. "Even more important, for the first time I saw what a good marriage looked like. It made me realize how important it is to marry the right person from the get-go."

Lamar turned to Justin, a question in his eyes. "Do you think that, too?"

Justin nodded as he toweled off Roamer. "Yes. My parents have a very strong and happy relationship." He smiled at Lamar then turned and caught Amanda's gaze. "Having that kind of love and commitment as a foundation makes for a very good marriage."

"And happy marriages," Amanda concluded softly, pleasantly surprised to find them all on the same page, "make happy families."

THAT EVENING, JUSTIN offered to let Amanda do her wash in the laundry room at the lodge. Given that the alternative was driving into town to use the coin laundry, Amanda took him up on it. As she expected, he wandered in eventually to talk to her.

"Thanks for talking so frankly with Lamar today."

"No problem." Trying not to notice how handsome he looked with his skin bronzed from the summer sun, Amanda smiled.

Justin came closer, inundating her with the intoxicating scent of his cologne. "I had no idea you had such a rough childhood."

Amanda turned her eyes from the hard contours of his chest beneath his short-sleeved white polo shirt. Lower still, beneath the hem of his cargo shorts, were tanned, muscular legs. Covered with a light sprinkling of hair, one shade darker than the chestnut hair on his head, they hinted at just what fine shape he was in.

Mouth dry, Amanda forced a smile. When she leaned over to stuff another handful of lingerie into the washing machine, she ignored the way his eyes trailed over the lace. "It happens. People survive the bad stuff. They move on." She swallowed, giving in to the ever-present urge to take a good, long look at him.

He lounged against the dryer, arms folded in front of him. His lips took on a downward tilt. "Which, in my case, wasn't so hard. Since I had a great childhood."

She knew he was from one of the most powerful clans in Texas—the McCabe family—but that was all she'd been told. "Born with a silver spoon in your mouth?" she quipped as she added a detergent suitable for delicate fabrics.

He watched her recap the bottle and set it aside. "Yes and no."

Amanda set the dials and started the machine. Enjoying the cool air of the lodge, she folded her arms across her middle. "You're either rich and pampered, bud, or you're not."

Justin grinned, the man in him responding to the womanly challenge in her. "I was well cared for, but I didn't have access to a lot of money. I had chores, the normal allowance for around here. Which made for plenty of incentive to go after a part-time job."

She wrapped her mind around that. "You worked when you were a student?"

His brilliant blue eyes continued to mesh with hers. "From the time I was fourteen."

"What did you do?"

He studied her for a long beat. "A lot of stuff, actually. I bussed tables at Sonny's Barbecue, took tickets at the movie theater, worked in a warehouse, loading boxes onto trucks." He exhaled. "My last two years of college, I got a part-time gig working in a CPA's office, which led to my first job after graduation with a big-ten accounting firm."

"Wow." Amanda became aware that this was beginning to feel more like a date than a casual conversation. "You are well-rounded."

The hint of a smile curved his lips, too. "And you...?"

"Never did anything but carpentry."

He inched closer. "As good as you are at that, you're also really great with kids. Especially the ones who haven't had it easy."

She stepped back. "It takes one to know one."

He stubbornly held his ground, gazing down at her. "It's more than that," he observed. "You have a natural ability to communicate. Just being near you seems to calm Lamar down."

Amanda shrugged. "You're good with him, too."

"Not as good as you."

She leaned against the washer and felt the vibration of the cycle against her spine. "It's not a competition, Justin."

"Good thing." He sighed in something akin to defeat. "Because if it were, no question, you'd win."

And that bothered him, Amanda noted. Probably because he wanted to excel at everything he did. Silence, and an aching awareness, stretched between them. Amanda felt compelled to remind him, "You know there are no perks that come with my presence here tonight or at any other time."

He nodded, accepting her boundary. For now, anyway. "How about we just be friends then?"

Amanda scoffed. Now who was kidding himself? She moved away from the vibrating machine. Looked him up and down. "You and I can't be just friends."

He lifted a dark brow. "Why not?"

Amanda was sure he knew, but she decided to demonstrate the pitfalls anyway. She smiled, gliding closer. Keeping her gaze locked with his, she said brazenly, "I'll show you why not."

Chapter Four

Amanda told herself she was just going to prove her point—that there was nothing real between them—when, truthfully, she wanted to satisfy the desire that had been building from the first moment she had set eyes on Justin McCabe.

It wasn't just that he was tall and strong, and rugged enough to make her feel all woman to his man. Or that he had a heart big as all Texas, a heart that would take in homeless dogs and kids who had lost their way.

It was the way Justin McCabe looked at her, as if she was all that he had ever wanted or dreamed he could have. It was the way he smiled at her, the protectiveness of his touch, the way he seemed to know exactly what she was thinking and feeling, that gave her the courage to rise up on tiptoe, wreathe her arms about his neck and press her lips to his.

It was, she thought wistfully, enough to make her close her eyes and revel in that first electric contact. To savor the intoxicating male taste of his lips, the heat and pressure of his kiss, and the feel of his body pressed intimately against hers.

He wanted her, too. She knew it. Felt it. Relished it. And that was why, more than anything, she had to break off the reckless embrace and pull away.

"Not so fast," Justin rasped, before she could even take a breath. Pulling her right back into his arms, he threaded his hand through her hair and lowered his lips to hers.

Justin had wanted to kiss Amanda for what seemed like an eternity; he just hadn't figured it would happen until the work on the ranch was complete.

However, her sexy move on him had changed all that, made it okay for *him* to kiss *her*. And kiss her he did, savoring the softness of her lips, the heat of her body, the womanly fragrance of her hair and skin. She was strong and lithe, beautiful and seductive, tender and kind. And he wanted her more than the rational part of him knew he should.

Which was why, when she broke off the kiss a second time he had to respect it. Had to lift his head and let her go. She was breathing hard—as was he. Her cheeks were pink, her lips damp. The sweet feminine scent of her dominated his senses.

"That," Amanda said, trembling with desire, "is why we can't be just friends. Because the physical attraction will get in the way."

He was willing to take it to the next level if she was. "So, maybe we should renegotiate our initial agreement… and be friends *and* lovers."

Amanda appeared amused but not really surprised by what he was proposing. "Lovers," she repeated in a whisper-soft voice. "You don't pull any punches, do you?"

Justin tucked a strand of silky blond hair behind her ear. "I'm honest about what I want, what I need."

Amanda released a quavering breath. "Then I will be, too." Her eyes narrowed. "And that won't work, either."

"Why not?"

She picked up her laundry basket and walked over to

the dryer. "First, men with families like yours don't get involved with women from backgrounds like mine."

He watched her bend over and pull her clothes from the machine. "You underestimate me and my family."

"Second," she pushed on, "I'm not the kind of gal who can love someone, and leave him and *not* feel bad about breaking his heart."

He grinned at her joking manner and responded in kind. "What if I tell you my heart won't be broken?" he quipped, having an idea what it would feel like to be invited into her bed, and then, just a short time later, summarily kicked out. It would be disappointing as hell to be that close to heaven and then lose it all.

Amanda arranged the clothes in her basket so the frilly undies were beneath her plain T-shirts. "What if I tell you that mine will?"

Silence fell between them. She could tell by the expression flitting across his handsome face that he was weighing the truth behind her teasing words. "You have a lot going on here, Justin. A lot to accomplish in just a few weeks."

As if he didn't know that. He folded his arms across his chest. "It'll get done a lot faster with you here helping me."

"And then I'll be helping my granddad—and his company—by moving on to the next rural gig. I don't want to miss you when I'm gone. I don't want to miss—" she rose up on tiptoe and lightly kissed his lips "—this." Backing away again, she finished with an earnest look, "So it's better we just not start."

"How is the job going?" Granddad asked later that evening over the phone.

"Good." Amanda paced the length of her travel trailer. Usually she loved her cozy little space. Tonight, since she'd finished her laundry and brought it back to put away in her limited storage space, she felt trapped and hemmed in.

"You sound…stressed."

How well her grandfather knew her. "I'm just tired," she fibbed.

"McCabe treating you well?"

Amanda stepped outside into the muggy heat of the night and gazed up at the star-filled Texas sky. She looked over at the lodge. The lights in Justin's office were on. He was probably still working on all the paperwork for those grants.

She rubbed her temples and continued pacing, thinking about the sweet sensuality of his embrace and her passionate reaction to it. "He's a reasonable client." Never pushing her to work too hard. Always wanting her to spend more time with him—as friends. When what she wanted was…

"And?" Her grandfather prodded, sensing there was more.

Amanda struggled to describe Justin without betraying her growing feelings. "He's the kind of man who takes on impossible challenges and sees them through. The kind who never got sent to the principal's office when he was growing up."

"A real role model, hmm?"

She heard the caution in her granddad's tone and felt it, too. "It appears that way," she admitted, telling herself that Justin was not like Rob in any way. Judging by his work on the ranch, when Justin committed to something or someone, he would not back away simply to make his life easier.

"From what I can gather, he's held in high esteem throughout the community, too. Generous. Kind…"

Granddad chuckled. "The same could be said about you, honey."

Amanda felt her halo begin to slip. Her granddad might

think she had grown up to be perfect, despite her teenage troubles. She knew otherwise.

"I'm sure Justin thinks you're amazing, too."

"At the moment, maybe," Amanda allowed with a sigh.

She couldn't help but think if she stayed around too long, she would do something that would demonstrate just how wrong she was for a guy like Justin.

She didn't want to see that look in his eyes, the one that said she'd let him down or somehow embarrassed him in front of his family. She didn't want to go back to feeling less than admirable. And the way to prevent that, she knew, was to stick to the tried and true. Her carpentry, life on the road, her devotion to her grandfather, and little more…

"But back to business," Amanda said, pushing her conflicted feelings aside. "How are things on your end, Granddad?"

"Busier than usual, that's for sure. I'll have to fill you in when you come home."

Amanda ducked back into the air-conditioned comfort of her trailer. "That sounds good." She let out a wistful sigh

Granddad paused; as always he read more of her thoughts than she would have liked. "You know, if you're tired of traveling, you could work here in San Angelo exclusively again."

She chuckled. "And miss out on all those high-paying gigs?" The ones that brought an extra cushion of solvency to the family business and made up for the overall loss of revenue as her grandfather made the transition into retirement.

"I understand why you took over for me after you ended your engagement to Rob, that you needed a change of scene," Granddad continued soberly. "But you don't have to keep running away."

Amanda harrumphed. This was an old argument, one

neither of them was likely to win. "I'm not running away, Granddad."

"Mmm-hmm. When I was sixty-eight, I would have believed you. Now that I'm seventy, I know better."

She laughed out loud. Leave it to her granddad to make a joke to break the tension. "I do miss you, Granddad," she said fondly.

"Then how about you come home this weekend? Spend a day or two in San Angelo so we can really talk."

Knowing that "conversation" would end up being a full inquisition into her current situation, Amanda hedged, "I'll have to see how things go work-wise, but maybe I will." Leaving the ranch and Justin—if just for a night—could put everything into perspective.

On the other hand, maybe rushing through to the end of this job was the best way to go. The sooner she stopped seeing Justin every day, the sooner she would stop risking another kiss. The sooner she would stop fantasizing about him.

Aware that her grandfather was waiting for an answer, Amanda said, "I'll just have to see."

She heaved a sigh of relief when he agreed to leave it at that.

"I SMELL THE bacon cooking, too, fellas," Justin told his canine companions at eight-thirty the next morning. "But you're out of luck because I don't have any to give you. And Amanda has not invited us to share."

All five dogs remained at the back door of the lodge, eyes looking up at him hopefully, tails wagging.

"We can't just barge in on her," Justin continued. "Especially since she started working before the sun was even up this morning and is now on a well-deserved meal break."

Professor whimpered with excitement. Roamer let out

a short, demanding bark. Then Sleepy, overwhelmed with excitement, began to sniff and circle. "Oh, no," Justin said. That was all he needed—a hot mess on the mudroom floor.

Swiftly grabbing Sleepy's collar before the dog could squat, Justin ordered sternly, "All right, fellas, I'm letting you out, but you stay with me." He gave the dogs the hand signal to heel and opened the back door.

To his relief, they stayed by his side.

He led the way down the steps to the grassy area favored by the dogs. Sleepy immediately got down to business. Woof followed suit. Professor sniffed the air and sprinted off.

His four friends darted in pursuit.

Muttering under his breath, Justin raced after them.

He caught up just as they reached the door to Amanda's trailer, where the tantalizing smells of freshly cooked bacon, waffles and strong coffee abounded.

Woof let out a loud bark. Then another. The rest joined in, and suddenly it was like the inside of a kennel. Justin put two fingers between his teeth and let out a long, sharp whistle. "Sit!" he commanded.

The trailer door opened and Amanda stepped out. Damned if she wasn't a sight for sore eyes, with her butterscotch-blond hair swept into a clip on the back of her head, cheeks flushed pink and her eyes glinting with humor. She wore a hot pink T-shirt and cream-colored overall shorts that showcased her long, tanned legs. On her feet were the steel-toed construction boots she wore when she worked.

She smelled like breakfast and warm maple syrup. It was clear, from the empty plate in her hand, that she had just finished eating. She mugged affectionately at the dogs, who were now sitting patiently in a semicircle, begging for scraps. She smiled at them, then turned to Justin. "Everything under control as usual, I see."

Her teasing hit the mark. "No kidding," Justin retorted drily.

His lovable mutts couldn't seem to stay away from her any more than he could. Chuckling, Amanda went inside and came back with crisp slices of bacon. She broke them into pieces and tossed a section to each dog.

They downed it quickly, licked their chops and stared at her as if in love. Justin knew how they felt. There was something captivating about her. Something that made him want to stand here and talk with her all day.

"I called the heating and air-conditioning company," he said. "The unit they were waiting on finally came in. They'll be out to hook up the bunkhouse HVAC today, so starting tomorrow you'll be able to work in air-conditioned comfort."

"That's nice."

"I feel bad you've had to work in such blistering conditions."

"That's okay, I'm used to the heat…it's nothing I can't handle. But thanks for thinking of me. I'm sure Lamar will appreciate it, too. Though he hasn't complained, I know he's not as used to working in the sweltering temperatures as I am."

Curious, he moved closer. "Are you going to need his help today?"

She met his gaze. "If you can spare him, I'd love it."

Justin nodded. Beside him, the dogs continued to pant and look at Amanda adoringly. "I'll send him over to help you as soon as he arrives." Could this conversation get any more inane?

"Thank you." She paused as her next thought hit. "Have you had breakfast yet?"

He grinned. Now they were getting somewhere. "Does a bowl of cereal at dawn count?"

Her smile broadened. "Hang on." She slipped inside the trailer. Half a minute later she returned with a foil-covered plate and quarter-full bottle of maple syrup. Breakfast to go. Not exactly what he'd had in mind...

Amanda handed the food over, being careful not to touch him during the transfer. "This will make us even," she said cheerfully, "since you cooked me dinner the other night."

Justin would have preferred to be invited in, even for a few minutes. But it was clear that wasn't going to happen. Amanda had set the boundaries the night before. She was going to maintain them whether he wanted her to or not.

AN HOUR LATER, Lamar had arrived and was hard at work helping Amanda. Justin was in his office compiling more data for the grant applications when he received a phone call from Libby Lowell-McCabe. She asked him to drive into town for a meeting at the Lowell Foundation offices, to discuss the particulars of the fund-raising dinner he was going to be hosting.

When Justin arrived, he was not surprised to see three of the Laramie Boys Ranch board members. They were a hands-on group. He greeted Miss Mim, the retired librarian and long-time community leader first, then social worker Mitzy Martin and finally Libby, the board's chairwoman.

Libby motioned for everyone to sit down then turned to Justin. "Do you want the good news first, or the bad?"

That was easy. "The good."

Libby smiled. "The guest list for the fund-raising dinner at the ranch is coming along nicely. We've got firm commitments from all the board members, plus reporters from the *Dallas Morning News* and the *Houston Chronicle,* and two TV news folks who are considering doing features on the ranch for their respective stations, as well as representatives from several major charitable foundations in Fort Worth and Corpus Christi."

Suddenly feeling the pressure mounting to make the event a success, Justin said, "So what's the bad news?"

"The only time we can get everyone together is Saturday evening."

Saturday. "As in tomorrow night?" Justin needed to make sure he understood.

Miss Mim lifted a hand. "We know it's short notice," she said quietly.

It wouldn't have been for any of them, Justin thought. The three women in the room could throw together a party on a moment's notice, and had done so plenty of times in the past year and a half as they toiled to turn the boys ranch from dream to reality.

"And probably very overwhelming for a guy," Mitzy Martin added kindly. "Which is why we're offering to do all the cooking and meal prep for you."

Irked to be thought of as incapable in any regard, Justin said, "That's not necessary. I can handle it."

Libby studied him. "You're sure? Because we really need the funds that publicity like this could bring in if we're going to expand the ranch anytime soon."

"I'll make sure all goes smoothly," Justin promised.

He and the three women talked some more about the event. They all approved his proposed menu. After Mitzy left to drive Miss Mim home, Justin stayed behind to talk to Libby. "How is the search going for counselors?"

Libby beamed. "We've located three husband-and-wife teams who would be perfect. I only wish we could build two more bunkhouses and hire them all."

So did Justin, but that would mean raising another million dollars, no easy feat. Especially since he had already donated the majority of his own inheritance to purchase the land and build the lodge. "What about the director position?"

Libby's expression grew conflicted, but she looked him in the eye. "We have a lot of qualified candidates with varied backgrounds. And we're looking at all of our options."

Which meant it probably wasn't going to be him. Disappointment knotted his gut. He leaned forward in his chair. "Am I still in the running?"

"Yes. Of course. You're the founder of the boys ranch, after all. If it weren't for you and your unwavering commitment—and the considerable funds you've put in—it wouldn't exist."

"And yet…?" Justin prodded, sensing there was something holding him back in their view.

Libby clasped her elegant hands together. "The board wants to make sure whoever holds the position can really relate to the kids and put him or herself in their shoes."

"Or in other words, you all think I won't be able to empathize enough with the kids to be effective."

Libby nodded reluctantly. "That pretty much sums it up, yes. I'm sorry, Justin."

First, Amanda basically—and erroneously—had told him he was out of her league, and now this. Justin wasn't sure he wanted to know what was next.

AMANDA WASN'T SURE what had happened with Justin at the board meeting in town. All she knew for certain was that his expression was unusually pensive when he walked into the bunkhouse kitchen to resume supervision of Lamar.

"So what do you think?" Lamar asked Justin proudly.

Justin surveyed the unfinished store-bought cabinets,

butcher-block countertops and newly laid wood floor. All had been perfectly leveled and installed with Lamar's help.

Eagerly, the teen stepped back to point out, "Adding the crown molding really makes the cabinets look a lot fancier, don't you think?"

Justin studied the clean, elegant edges and turned back to Lamar with approval. "You guys did a really nice job. The whole thing looks custom-built."

"Or at least it will when we get everything stained and varnished," Amanda said with a smile.

Justin smiled back at her. "So what's next?" he asked, coming nearer.

"We'll build the bookcases and wall lockers in each of the bedrooms. And of course we'll make sure those are nicely trimmed, too. Then we'll add the cabinets to all the bathrooms."

Justin's eyes locked on hers. "Can you have at least one bedroom and bath done by Saturday evening?"

It would be pushing it, but since it seemed so important, Amanda nodded. "Sure," she said. "Although nothing will be varnished yet."

"That's okay." One corner of his mouth quirked as he turned back to Lamar. "I'm going to need some extra help tomorrow for a fund-raising dinner, here at the ranch. I know it's Saturday, typically you get that time off, but I would appreciate it if you could help out with the preparations, serving and cleanup. Of course, any hours you put in will count toward your community service."

Justin's tone was amenable, yet Lamar was wary. Probably, Amanda thought, because he worried he would be out of his element and end up falling flat on his face.

"What exactly would I have to do?" Lamar asked nervously.

Justin either missed or chose to ignore the teen's unease.

"A little of everything, probably." He brushed off further questions, assuring, "We'll figure it out as we go."

Famous last words, Amanda thought.

"In the meantime—" Justin paused to check his phone and punch in something on his keyboard "—I've got to get a list together and go back into town to buy groceries. I need your help for that, too." He slid his phone back into his pocket.

Lamar dug in his heels. "I'm helping Amanda," he protested.

Realizing that tempers were about to flare once again, Amanda put a soothing hand on the teen's shoulder. "It's okay, Lamar. I'm just going to be measuring and cutting wood this afternoon. There's still plenty for you to help me with the next few weeks, when Justin doesn't need you to assist him."

Lamar relaxed beneath her maternal touch and reluctantly acquiesced. Justin smiled with relief and the two guys strode off. Fifteen minutes later, they got into Justin's truck and drove away.

Amanda went back to work.

While they were gone, she wondered how it was going.

She found out when they returned.

The moment Justin cut the motor, Lamar stormed out of the pickup and started for Amanda.

Justin followed. "Lamar. Come back here."

As out of control as Justin was in control, Lamar spun around to shout, "Why should I? You don't want me around. Admit it! You're just doing this 'cause you have to, same as me!"

"You're wrong about that, Lamar," Justin replied.

But, Amanda could see, Lamar didn't believe him. In fact, wouldn't have believed anyone at that point.

All five dogs, who had been hanging out on the porch of

the lodge, stood and came forward, tails at half-mast. They seemed to be as concerned about Lamar's upset state as Amanda. She took off her goggles and gloves, set them on the table and walked toward the guys. "How about I give you fellas a hand? I imagine there's a lot of stuff to unload."

When Lamar looked over at her, the fight seemed to seep out of him. He ducked his head and moved for the truck's rear doors.

There were a lot of groceries, Amanda noted. Cases of sparkling water, soda and tea. Butcher-paper-wrapped meat. Four gourmet pies from the Sugar Love bakery. Fresh vegetables, fruits and herbs. Together, the three of them carried everything in and set it on the counter.

Lamar still wouldn't look Justin in the eye. "Now can I take a break?" he bit out before Justin could say anything more. "I didn't even have lunch, you know!"

At that, Justin looked completely taken aback.

Once again, Amanda felt compelled to intervene. She placed a comforting arm around Lamar's thin shoulders, not sure why, just knowing the kid brought out the mother in her. "I've got some sandwiches already made in the fridge in my trailer," she told the teen lightly, noticing he was near tears and struggling to hide it. "Why don't you go cool off and help yourself to a few of those? There are chips and apples, too."

Lamar's grateful expression reminded her just how downtrodden he was. "Thanks, Amanda." He pivoted and left the lodge, pausing only long enough to pat the dogs on the porch before crossing the lawn.

Amanda turned back to Justin, sensing he needed comforting, too. "I'm assuming you didn't have lunch, either," she remarked drily.

Broad shoulders slumping, he scrubbed a hand over his eyes. "You're right. I didn't."

"We could take care of the stuff here, wait a minute and then both go over and join Lamar."

He exhaled and shot her a gruff look. "I appreciate the way you're able to calm Lamar down, but you don't have to take care of us."

It was the first time he'd rebuffed her help. She found it—and him—oddly fascinating. Unable to help herself, she stepped closer. "I do if I want to coexist in peace." She emptied produce from a bag. "What happened at the store, anyway?"

Justin grimaced. "I wrote out a list for Lamar of stuff I figured would be easy to find." Justin reached into the pocket of his jeans and brought out a crumpled-up piece of paper. "Another for me, with the harder stuff, like fresh basil."

That sounded fine. "And then?"

"We each took a cart and then…nothing." Justin opened the fridge and set the meat on a shelf, the vegetables in the crisper. "I'm done with my list, and I look around…and where is he?" Justin continued, clearly exasperated. "The magazine rack, looking at motorcycles!"

Amanda stepped in to hand Justin the rest of the refrigerator items. "He didn't get anything on the list?" she asked in dismay.

"Nope." Justin shook his head. "Not a single item. He didn't even have his basket with him anymore."

Unable to understand this—Lamar was always so helpful when he was with her—Amanda scrunched up the plastic bags and put them in the recycling container. "What did he say when you asked him about it?"

Justin lounged against the counter, arms folded in front of him, his big body simmering with pent-up frustration. "That he's no good at grocery shopping and shouldn't be required to do it."

That sounded like the contemptuous, passive-aggressive kid who had been sentenced to community service. Eager to hear the entire story, Amanda settled next to Justin. "And you said?"

"I'll help you. We'll start with the olive oil and the butter." Justin shook his head. "But he wouldn't cooperate there, either. Wouldn't even give a half effort. All he would do is stand in front of whatever shelf I directed him to, and look at the packages, and sometimes pick something. Never, of course, what we were looking for."

Amanda wished she could reach out and comfort Justin without it being misconstrued. "He was probably just angry because you reprimanded him in public."

Glance narrowing, Justin met her gaze. "I wasn't reprimanding him. I was just trying to get him back on task."

Amanda chided, "Trust me. People know when you're not happy." He had a very expressive face, very expressive eyes, a very willful nature. Only right now, that strong will wasn't helping.

Justin winced and scoured a hand over his jaw. He hadn't shaved yet today. The resulting stubble gave him a very rugged, masculine look she itched to explore. Mistaking the reason for her silence, he finally muttered, "I suppose you could have done a better job?"

She wasn't about to lie, but didn't want to rub it in, either. "That's really not the point, is it?" She gave him a long, level look. "You're the one running this ranch."

"For now." Frown lines bracketed his sensual lips. He came another step closer. "It may not be for much longer, if I can't even get through to one kid in need."

"Give it time," Amanda advised. "In the meantime, try an apology. Trust me on this, Justin. A few kind words of compassion can work wonders."

Justin gathered her close. He wrapped both his arms

around her middle. "For me, too," he admitted in a low voice.

His mouth was so close she could feel the heat of his breath on her forehead. "What do you mean?"

He rubbed his thumb across her lower lip, tracing its shape. His eyes took on a sexy shimmer. "It helps having you here with me. More than you know."

The tenderness of his voice obliterated her defenses even more. "Justin—"

He tunneled his hands through her hair and lifted her face to his. The sound of his husky laughter warmed her heart. "Just one kiss, Amanda. That's all I'm asking." He gave her no chance to refuse.

At the first touch of his lips to hers, Amanda splayed her hands across his chest. She swore to herself she wasn't going to yield to temptation, but before even a second had gone by, her lips had parted under the seductive pressure of his. Her knees weakened and her heartbeat sped up. Wild longing swept through her. And suddenly she was kissing him back with all the wonder and affection in her heart. By the time the possessive caress ended, she was tingling from head to toe. And worse, on the verge of falling harder and faster for Justin than she ever dreamed possible.

Scared by what that could mean, she pushed away from the unyielding hardness of his body. "Justin. We can't do this."

He frowned, perplexed, then reluctantly stepped back.

"You have to concentrate on helping Lamar now," Amanda reiterated firmly. "And nothing else."

As much as he hated to admit it, Justin knew that Amanda was right. The main goal was to make Lamar feel good about himself, to put him in situations where he would thrive, not struggle. Ashamed he had lost sight of that, even for a short while, Justin went in search of the boy.

In not acting swiftly enough, he had failed Billy. He would not do the same to Lamar.

Luckily, it didn't take Justin too long to find the missing teen. He was sitting in Amanda's trailer, all five canines sprawled on the floor at his side. A half-eaten sandwich and a nearly full bag of chips was spread out on the table. For someone who had professed to be starving, he didn't appear to have much of an appetite. "Got room for one more?" Justin asked.

Lamar just looked at him and sulked.

Justin slid into the banquette across from him, ready to do what he hadn't done before. "I'm sorry if I was a little short with you back at the store," he said sincerely.

"Yeah, well," Lamar admitted reluctantly, "I probably should have tried a little harder to find some of that stuff, even if I didn't know what half of it was."

Justin took the admission for the peace offering it was. He helped himself to a chip. "That's good to hear. But you need to know that my grouchiness had nothing to do with you. I was ticked off because the ladies on the board of directors don't think I can pull off this party because I'm a man, and I realized when I was in there, trying to buy all this stuff, that they're probably right."

He retrieved a sandwich from Amanda's fridge and sat down to unwrap it. "The truth is, I don't know what I'm doing. I mean, I can cook guy food till the sun comes up. But a dinner party?" Justin forced himself to take a bite. He swallowed and squinted at Lamar. "As much as I hate to admit it, they're right. I am out of my league. Way out of my league."

Lamar picked up his sandwich and began to eat. "Then why do it?"

"Because if I don't, I won't get the job I want, and I really want to be the director of the Laramie Boys Ranch."

"Why?"

"Because I know I have what it takes to run the place and help kids just like you. And I want to be given the chance to try."

Lamar munched on his sandwich and thought about that for a long moment. "They really said you couldn't do this because you were *a guy?*"

"Yep."

Lamar slammed a palm on the table. "Well, that's just *wrong.*"

Justin chuckled, aware this was the first time in his life he'd been subject to gender discrimination. On the job, anyway. "My opinion exactly."

Lamar went to the fridge. He took out two apples and tossed one to Justin. "I don't know a lot about that stuff, either, but I can probably learn." He sat down opposite Justin. "I mean, heck, I'm learning carpentry pretty quick."

Justin polished off his sandwich and started on his apple. "You sure are."

Lamar leaned forward enthusiastically. "Just tell me what you need, and I'll do my best to deliver. And Justin? Thanks for apologizing." Lamar swallowed, seeming suddenly emotional. "It means a lot to hear someone besides me say 'I'm sorry.'"

AMANDA WAS BACK at work when she saw Lamar and Justin come out of the trailer a short time later. One look at their body language told her they were no longer at odds. Consequently, Lamar assisted Justin at the lodge for the rest of the day. Relieved that things seemed to be going better, Amanda kept to herself, working late into the evening. Given how long the lodge lights were on Friday night,

Justin was burning the midnight oil, too, getting ready for the fund-raiser.

She was tempted to pop in and see how things were going, but mindful of her refusal to be drafted into catering and cohosting duties by a man she found extraordinarily attractive, she stayed away.

Justin, she was sure, would do fine without her. And if he didn't, it really wasn't her problem. Even if it inexplicably *felt* like her problem...

Eventually, she went to sleep, only to dream of Justin, and the kiss they had shared, all night long. Frustrated, and knowing she couldn't allow it to happen again or she really would fall hard for him, she got out of bed and started her day early.

Lamar was back bright and early Saturday morning.

On track to finish building one bookcase and wall-mounted wooden locker as promised, Amanda labored in the bunkhouse all morning. Lamar hosed down the porch, cut and edged the grass, and could be seen going in and out of the lodge all day long. Justin did not appear.

At five, she had completed the installation of the bathroom cabinets, and was finished for the day. Not sure what she was going to do during the fund-raising party—maybe go into town, see a movie or drive to San Angelo and see her grandfather—she headed for her trailer and a quick shower.

She had just put on clean clothes and run a comb through her hair, when she heard footsteps outside her trailer. "Amanda!" Lamar pounded on her door, his voice frantic. "It's an emergency! You've got to come quick!"

Chapter Five

Amanda raced after Lamar, her heart pounding. The dogs were running back and forth across the deck at the rear of the lodge. The unpleasant smell of something burning scented the air. "What happened?"

"You'll see." Lamar darted up the steps. Amanda followed him through the lodge and into the kitchen.

A grim-faced Justin stood next to the stove. In front of him were two big charred pieces of still-smoking meat. Aghast, Amanda could only stare.

His expression hardened. "I didn't hear the timer go off."

"Now what are we going to do?" Lamar cried, acting as if this were a disaster of the first magnitude.

"What we're *not* going to do is panic." Amanda turned back to Justin, who was still standing there looking like he wanted to punch something. Preferably himself.

"How long before guests arrive?"

His dark gaze got even darker. "Less than an hour."

Still shoving his hands through his hair and racing back and forth, Lamar reported, "And the main part of dinner is all burned!"

Amanda knew how much was riding on this—for the ranch, the prospective kids and Justin personally. Not to mention the fact that Lamar needed a "win."

"Now, now, let's stay calm," she soothed, moving closer

to inspect the charred beef. Her many years in the kitchen had given her lots of experience in fixing unexpected culinary mishaps. Ignoring Justin's bleak expression, she switched on the exhaust over the stove. "Lamar, can you open a few windows and go to the bunkhouse and bring in one of the big floor fans? We've got to get the smoky smell out of here."

"Sure." Glad to be part of the solution, Lamar dashed off, opening windows in the dining area as he went.

His body tense with disappointment, Justin opened the heavy window above the kitchen sink and then turned to her. "Look, I appreciate you coming over," he told her, with a shake of his head. "But there's nothing you can do to rescue this. It's my screwup. I'll be accountable."

A wave of unexpected empathy wafted through Amanda. This was one time when her history of cleaning up after her own failures, of which there were many, would come in handy. One time when she could show Justin a thing or two…

Refusing to be dragged down by his sour mood, she mugged at him playfully. "Oh, ye of little faith!" She cut a deep slit in the center of the scorched beef tenderloin and checked out what was left. "See?" She elbowed him, prompting him to look. "Inside, the meat is still quite edible. All we have to do is cut off the burned part and see what we have to work with."

Justin reluctantly stripped down one hunk of charred beef, while she did the other. By the time they had finished cutting off the barklike crust, they had a good two pounds of nice, tender high-quality beef that smelled as if it had done time in a smoker, not such a bad thing when it came to Southwestern-style cuisine.

Justin studied the remains and rubbed a hand across the tense muscles at the back of his neck. He saw the value in salvaging the edible meat. "Unfortunately, that's not enough to feed fourteen people."

Amanda set the burnt pieces aside for later disposal. "It is if we turn it into something else, like beef barbacoa enchiladas."

Justin gave her a steady look that sent heat spiraling through her. She had the feeling that if the situation hadn't been so dire he would have swept her off her feet and kissed her. Suddenly, hope glimmered in his eyes. "Do you know how to make that?"

Amanda pushed aside her earlier decision not to get involved with this dinner. The future of the ranch—which could help a lot of boys like Lamar—was at stake. She thought about all the times she and her gran had cooked for her granddad and his buddies when they gathered to play poker or watch sports on TV. "I do. Plus, I have all the ingredients we need in my kitchen."

While Justin worked on shredding the beef into bite-size pieces, Amanda and Lamar strode back to her trailer. They returned with their arms full of groceries and two large glass baking pans. Using dried chiles and chicken stock, she quickly whipped up a red sauce.

While Lamar stirred the bubbling sauce, she softened the tortillas and diced two onions. She showed both guys how to put a spoonful of meat into the center of the softened tortilla, and add a teaspoon of onion, before rolling them and putting them seam-side down in the baking pan. She covered the rolled enchiladas with the red sauce and a sprinkling of crumbled *queso fresco*.

"What are we going to serve with it, though?" Justin asked.

Good question. "What were you going to have?"

"Roasted vegetables." Justin pulled baking sheets out of the fridge, and showed her the sliced squash, zucchini, onions and baby carrots, all ready to cook. "And field greens with buttermilk dressing."

"That's all good. It'll work nicely with the enchiladas."

Justin breathed a sigh of relief, as did Lamar. Amanda smiled. Whether the two guys knew it or not, they really were becoming a team.

"Any appetizers?" she asked.

Justin opened up the fridge again. He brought out several nicely prepared serving platters. On them were water crackers with blue cheese and walnut spread, stuffed mushrooms—which had yet to be baked—and chilled shrimp with cocktail sauce.

"All would have been perfect as a prelude to beef tenderloin," Amanda observed thoughtfully.

"That's what the book on entertaining said." Justin paused. "But none of that goes with enchiladas, does it?"

"Let me think." Amanda studied the repast. "The shrimp will be okay if we add a little lime juice and cilantro to the cocktail sauce. We can quickly make fresh guacamole and *pico de gallo* to top the water crackers, or substitute chips for the crackers, if you prefer. What's in the stuffed mushrooms?"

"Cream cheese, breadcrumbs." Justin looked at Lamar, who dutifully supplied, "Other stuff…"

Amanda laughed. When Justin produced the recipe, she glanced at it. "I think this will probably be okay." It wasn't Southwestern, but it was neutral enough in flavor to accompany the spicier dishes.

"So we're good?" Justin asked.

Amanda nodded. "I think so."

With less than twenty minutes to go before the guests arrived, Lamar chopped up the burned meat and carried it out to the dogs, who were delighted with their savory treat. Justin worked on cleaning up the lodge kitchen, and

Amanda returned to her trailer to prepare the *pico de gallo* and guacamole.

By the time Justin came over to assist, she was done. Noting once again how small and intimate her space seemed with the big, handsome Texan in it, she handed him large bowls of both dips, along with a fresh bag of tortilla chips. With a tingle of awareness sifting through her, Amanda gulped in a bolstering breath and kept her mind on his goal—which was to entertain successfully that evening.

She flashed a brisk smile, meant to demonstrate just how emotionally uninvolved she was. "Here you go. You should be all set. Oh! And I wrote down the temperature and time for the enchilada bake. You'll want it to finish about ten minutes before you plan to serve the main course, so it will have time to set."

A mixture of tenderness and gratitude dominated his handsome features. "I don't know how to thank you."

Aware she had to find the strength to keep her guard up now that the crisis was averted, she swallowed and moved away. "I realize this was a singular occurrence."

He tracked her with his eyes. "It doesn't have to be."

Oh, how she wished that were the case.

The sound of a car motor—make that multiple motors—could be heard coming up the driveway.

"I hope it goes well."

Justin caught her wrist. "Come to dinner."

A jolt of electricity coursed through her as his warm fingers grazed her skin. But, out of an increasing need for self-preservation, she slipped from his light, beseeching grasp and stepped away. She held the door open for him to exit her trailer. "I couldn't."

Reluctantly, he moved to leave, strong arms full. "Even as my guest?"

Amanda knew he wanted her there. Obviously, as culinary backup, to help with the dinner. To make sure all went smoothly with the rest of the cooking and serving. And yes, he was grateful for her assistance and happy with her now. But one day, he might not be. Especially if his family—who were pillars of the community—did not approve of him getting involved with a woman from the wrong side of the tracks.

"You have to go," she said urgently, telling herself that if they were lucky they could one day be casual friends. And only casual friends.

Justin gave her another look that indicated there would have been a lot more persuading on his part were the guests not already parking their cars and trucks. Then they heard the sounds of doors slamming, voices filling the air.

"And good luck tonight." Amanda would be thinking of him—and Lamar—whether she wanted to or not.

AMANDA WAS TRYING to figure out how to make her getaway—not an easy feat since the driveway was filled with a dozen vehicles—when her cell phone rang. She picked up, happy for the distraction. The last thing she needed to be doing was standing here thinking about how it would have felt to be Justin's cohost—or date—on an evening such as this. "Hey, Granddad." Amanda smiled.

"Hey there yourself, sweetheart," A.B.'s voice rumbled over the phone. "I haven't heard a lot from you the past few days, so I thought I'd check in, see how the job is going."

"Oh. Great," Amanda was able to say truthfully.

"You need any more help? I can always come out to assist."

Amanda knew that bored tone. Her grandfather was feeling hemmed in. Unfortunately, there'd been a role reversal in their relationship. Now, she was the one looking out for him. "Doc Parsons said no more traveling jobs, remember? You're supposed to be phasing into retirement. Which means you can continue to *run* your business as long as you don't do the carpentry work, too!"

"Yeah, yeah, yeah…" Granddad harrumphed. Moving on, as always, when the talk got too uncomfortable, he said, "So, you're good?"

Was she? Talk about a loaded question! How all right could a woman be when she spent all her private time yearning for a man who was off-limits to her? But leery of letting her granddad know that, Amanda adapted her usual cocky attitude. "I'm fine. That foster kid I told you about is helping me part of the time."

"How is he working out?"

"Nicely," she reflected fondly. "Lamar seems to have a natural talent for carpentry."

"Maybe you can recruit him to apprentice with you, once he graduates from high school."

If Lamar graduated from high school, Amanda thought. To her grandfather, she admitted, "I've been thinking the same thing."

"Then?"

"I'll talk to him about it when the time is right."

"Everything else okay?"

She felt herself getting defensive. "Why wouldn't it be?"

"You tell me. I have a feeling you've got something on your mind."

Make that some*one,* Amanda thought, looking out her trailer window and watching the guests move from the lodge over to the bunkhouse, en masse, the dogs bringing up the rear. Finally, she said in the most offhand manner she could manage, "There's a fund-raising thing going on at the ranch tonight."

"Ah." A.B. knew how uncomfortable things like that made her, especially when they involved the movers and shakers of Texas society.

"If you need a break, why not do what I suggested earlier and come on home tonight? I've already made plans to go out and play poker this evening, but we could have breakfast tomorrow. Maybe see a movie in the afternoon."

That sounded good. Anything to get her mind off Justin. And Lamar. And whether or not this dinner would help raise the funds the ranch so desperately needed to continue expanding.

The truth was, she missed her grandfather. Missed his steady, reassuring presence. Amanda smiled, already feeling better. "Okay, Granddad, I will. I'll see you later, okay?"

"Travel safe." A.B. ended the call.

She slid her cell phone into her purse. She'd just found her keys when a rap sounded on her door. It was Lamar. He was grinning from ear to ear this time, clearly in the flush of victory. "Amanda! You've got to come over to the bunkhouse and tell them all about the stuff you've been teaching me. The reporters especially are really impressed."

Amanda could have passed on the opportunity to sing her own praises, but she wasn't about to let Lamar lose the chance to feel good about himself and what he had accomplished. She looked down at her sleeveless navy blouse, knee-length khaki walking shorts and flats. Thought about changing into something more on par with the dresses and sport coats the guests were all wearing, and decided what the heck. She was who she was. And she wasn't a guest. There was no sense in pretending she was one of them.

She set her purse, phone and keys aside, and walked out with Lamar.

"AND LAMAR HELPED you with all of this?" Wade McCabe asked, clearly impressed, as he and the other guests examined the quality of the kitchen cabinet installation.

Glad Wade seemed to be coming around to what his son was trying to accomplish here, Amanda nodded. She had seen how much it meant to Justin to have his father's approval. "Lamar also helped cut and add the trim that gives the cupboards a more custom look. And, of course, all the woodwork in the bunkhouse will be finished with stain and a finish that will feel silky to the touch."

"I'm going to help with that, too," Lamar proclaimed. Catching himself, he said, "That is, if Amanda agrees."

Catching Mitzy's knowing glance, Amanda smiled and added hastily, "I'd welcome the help if it's okay with the boss."

She didn't want anyone—especially the social worker in charge of Lamar's case—thinking she was undercutting Justin's supervision of the teenager.

Justin nodded his approval. "As far as I'm concerned, the more Lamar learns, the better." His customary confidence back, he winked at Amanda. "Especially since he has such a great teacher."

"I have a great student," she replied. Lamar beamed. The group was all smiles as they headed back toward the ranch house.

Libby fell into step beside Amanda. "Have dinner with us," she urged.

Amanda looked at the chairwoman of the board. "Thank you." She appreciated the sincere invitation. "But I'm really not dressed."

Libby glanced at her own cotton sheath, then back at Amanda's knee-length shorts and blouse. "Nonsense! You look great. And if we're to make this ranch all it can be, we really need your input, as well as Lamar's."

JUSTIN WASN'T SURPRISED that Amanda had been asked to dine with them. He'd issued the same invitation for all the same reasons. He was surprised she agreed, but once she did Lamar felt comfortable enough to join them, as well.

Both fielded a lot of questions throughout the meal. Amanda talked about learning the art of carpentry. Lamar discussed how much he liked being at the ranch and learning a trade that might someday turn into a job. The ranch was *much* different than school.

There, it was all about grades, the future and the pressure to get stuff done. At the ranch, when he was with Amanda, it was all about being in the moment. He admitted he was hoping Justin would let him keep on working there, even after his community service was finished.

Justin spoke about their plans to expand the facility one bunkhouse at a time. Costs were discussed next. Justin detailed the various ways they had been able to limit building and construction expenses, without sacrificing comfort or quality.

By the time the reporters and most of the board members, including his father, had left, Justin was certain the project would be getting positive press, as well as donations from the charitable foundations present that evening. Best of all, he'd begun to feel like he could finally put what had happened with Billy completely behind him.

The board members were pleased, too.

"I can't tell you how happy I am to see you doing so well here," Mitzy remarked to Lamar as she helped to clear away the dessert dishes.

Libby nodded agreement. "I never saw the 'before' attitude, but you are obviously thriving in your community service here."

"It's pretty easy with Amanda—and Justin—around," Lamar said shyly.

"That's good to hear." Mitzy put the plates in the dishwasher and smiled again. "Dinner was great, by the way. Although I am curious." She turned to Justin. "Why did you change your mind about the menu? We thought you were cooking whole beef tenderloins."

"He was until he screwed up and burned the meat," Lamar blurted out. "But then Amanda saved the day and showed us how to make enchiladas and change around the other stuff so it would go with it, and… Uh-oh." Lamar turned pale. "Was I not supposed to say that?"

Justin held up a hand, not the least bit upset. "Lamar's right," he said. "Amanda did save the day."

Flushing self-consciously, Amanda shook off the praise. "It wasn't that big a deal."

Justin was determined to give her the accolades she deserved. "Nonsense." He turned to their two remaining guests. "Dinner would have been a disaster had Amanda not stepped in at the last minute to help us."

Libby and Mitzy exchanged approving smiles. "Well, then, thank you again for being so charitable," Libby told Amanda.

She wished more credit was going to Justin—after all, he was the one who had founded the ranch and worked so hard to make it happen. "I'm all for good causes. And the boys ranch is definitely one of them."

The cleanup and conversation continued until almost midnight.

Still chattering about how much he loved the ranch, Lamar hitched a ride back to town with Mitzy and Libby.

Justin and Amanda were alone once again.

Which, considering how attracted she was to the evening's host, was perhaps not such a good thing.

Taking a deep breath, she stepped away from the driveway and onto the grass.

A full moon and stars shone in the velvety-dark Texas sky, and a warm summer breeze blew across their bodies. It couldn't have been a more romantic setting, which was why, Amanda knew, she had to bid the handsome man beside her adieu.

She slid her hands into the pockets of her shorts, broke away from the quiet intensity of his gaze and took off in the direction she needed to go. "I better head back to my trailer."

Justin caught up with her in three quick strides. He slid a protective hand beneath her elbow. "Let me walk you."

She tingled at the protectiveness of his touch. For both their sakes, she eased away. "Really," she reiterated firmly, working hard to keep their mutual attraction at bay. "It isn't necessary."

This time he kept his distance, even as he walked companionably beside her. "I know that." He sent her a gallant look. "I want to do it."

They continued across the grass. It felt like the end of a date. It wasn't a date. She had to remember that. Struggling to maintain her composure, Amanda looked up at him as they reached her trailer. "I know you're grateful for my help this evening…" she began.

He tilted his head to one side. "Very grateful." His voice slid over her like a caress.

"But it doesn't mean anything other than I was being neighborly," Amanda insisted.

His gaze swept over her before returning with patient deliberation to her eyes. "Good to know."

It astounded her, realizing how much she yearned to kiss—and make love—with him. "So…?"

Tenderness glimmered in his expression. "It still means a lot to me. You were a huge help tonight with the fundraising."

"I didn't do anything other than tell the truth."

His lips took on a seductive curve. "Then how about telling it now?"

Amanda lifted her chin, her heart thudding in her chest. She ignored the tingling sensation in her middle. "I don't know what you mean."

"Yes, Amanda, you do."

Amanda glanced at him, trying to figure out how to persuade him otherwise. Inside the trailer, her phone rang. She frowned and looked at her watch. At this hour, there was only one person it would be. "Hang on. I've got to get that."

She stepped inside her trailer and picked up her cell phone. "Hi, Granddad. Um, no." She paused, listening. "It's a long story. Suffice it to say, I got distracted working on something here, and before I knew it time got away from me." She paused again, aware Justin could probably hear every word she was saying. "Um, I don't think so. How about I call you tomorrow? Yes."

She said goodbye to her grandfather and walked back outside. Justin was standing, legs apart, hands braced on his waist, surveying the ranch. The quintessential cowboy. Only he wasn't a cowboy. And he didn't have a hat.

He pivoted to her, concern etched on the rugged planes of his face. "Everything okay?"

Wondering what it would be like to come home to a man like him every night for the rest of her life, Amanda said, "That was my grandfather. I had told him I was going to drive to San Angelo this evening and spend the rest of the weekend with him. Only…"

"You got caught up helping me."

Amanda breathed in, wishing Justin didn't smell and look so damn good. "Right."

"Are you going to see him tomorrow?"

"I'm not sure."

"You've got the day off."

It wasn't that. It was that the moment Granddad saw her, and asked her even a few questions, he would know she had feelings for Justin. And since her grandfather had no qualms about inserting himself into her love life, particularly if he thought she needed protecting...

Emotion roiled through her. She did not want the situation getting any more uncomfortable than it already was. "I'll think about it, okay?"

Justin watched her, as if knowing she was still keeping a lot more to herself than she was telling him.

"Anyway, back to what we were talking about..." Amanda started.

His irises darkened to the color of midnight as he listened intently to what she had to say.

"Just because we worked well as a team tonight, and have done a pretty good job getting Lamar back on track, doesn't mean we should read anything else into it."

The air was suddenly still enough to hear a pin drop. "Like attraction," he said.

Their gazes collided. "Right."

He moved subtly closer and flashed her a grin, all confident male. "Except I am attracted to you, Amanda."

And not afraid to face it.

She held up a staying hand. "And I'm attracted to you, too, Justin, but..."

Slowly, purposefully, his eyes locked on hers, he invaded her personal space. "But what?" he asked huskily.

She shivered when his hands lightly cupped her shoulders. "But there's a lot more than the physical component to a relationship, and I want a relationship, Justin." She lifted her chin. "The kind that lasts."

He lifted his broad shoulders. "So do I." His voice was

silky-soft, contemplative. And somehow dangerous in a deeply sensual way.

Panic welled, along with desire. Ignoring the fluttering of her pulse, she advised coolly, "Then you should pick more wisely."

Justin used his leverage on her to bring her closer still. Smiling, he said, "I am."

Chapter Six

Amanda knew it was a mistake to get so involved with Justin and this ranch when she was only going to be here a short time. It was an even bigger folly to let herself get emotionally attached to him. But she couldn't seem to help it. Whenever he looked at her that way, touched her, took her face into his hands and bent down and kissed her, all her resistance fled.

Her heart was wide-open. And what her heart wanted, she reluctantly admitted to herself, was him.

Amanda followed his lead and opened her mouth to the insistent, warm pressure of his. He kissed her again, harder, deeper. She moaned as his tongue swept the inside of her mouth. Another ribbon of desire unfurled inside her. Eager for more, she wrapped her arms around his shoulders and clasped him to her.

He pinned her against the side of the trailer, his body hard and muscular and hot. So hot. Something unexpectedly wanton was unleashed inside her. She moaned again and he continued kissing her with that mixture of confidence and tenderness that completely undid her. Trembling and aching to be filled, she arched against him. She could feel his heart pounding against her chest. And still it wasn't enough.

All restraint fled. His hands slid lower to cup her bottom, ardently holding her against the proof of his own mounting desire. She melted against him, surrendering to the erotic thrill of being held in his arms—to him. And damned if he didn't take her up on her offer.

"Amanda," he whispered against her mouth. He lifted his head, his eyes dark and hungry. "Stop me if you're going to," he said, his voice raspy and low. "Because if you don't…"

She didn't care what they had promised each other before. All that mattered was what she felt now.

"I don't want to stop you," she whispered back. She didn't want to stop any of this.

Taking him by the hand, she led him inside her trailer.

Their eyes met again. They kissed their way through her kitchen, past the bath and to the queen-size bed. Arms around each other, they tumbled, laughing, onto the mattress.

Justin rolled onto his back, tugging her over him, and kissed her again. And again. As if kissing were an art in and of itself. And heavens, Amanda noted blissfully, did the man know how to kiss! He stroked and invaded, tempted and caressed, adored and seduced, until nothing mattered but this moment, this night, and the two of them.

JUSTIN HAD WANTED Amanda since the first second he'd set eyes on her. That wanting had grown exponentially with every moment since. She'd wanted him, too, even though she'd tried to hide it beneath her confident, independent demeanor. But with her lithe, hot body sprawled on top of him, their legs intimately entangled, there was no more pretending.

Her nipples were taut. Her breath, erratic.

Rock-hard, he rolled her onto her back and turned his attention to unbuttoning her blouse, gently removing it and then her bra. She watched, with a look as sweet as heaven, as he bent to her breasts and kissed the pale orbs and rosy tips. "Damn, but you're gorgeous," he breathed, disrobing her the rest of the way.

She was soft all over, feminine. Just as he'd known she would be. A perfect breast in each hand, he kissed her languidly. She wrapped her legs around his waist, and kissed him back.

With her help, and a little more laughter from both of them, they were undressed in a minute flat. Then all amusement faded as she fisted both hands in his hair, sighed his name, and kissed him once again. Deeply. Passionately. Irrevocably.

The knowledge that she wanted him just as much as he wanted her sent another surge of heat soaring through him. Justin slid down her body, stroking her beautiful breasts, the deliciously flat plane of her stomach, the sensitive sweep of her lower abdomen, her smooth thighs. Homing in on the most womanly part of her, he sought out every sweet sensitive spot, until at last she gasped, lifted herself to him, and came apart with an exultant cry.

The depth of her satisfaction lit a fire beneath his own need.

He found the condom that had been in his wallet since he didn't know when. Their gazes caught for a long moment and the air between them hummed with anticipation and the yearning for more. Her hands trembling slightly, she helped him put it on, and then they were entwined in each other's arms again.

When she kissed him, it felt as though he'd been welcomed home. He had his mouth on hers and his hands beneath her hips, first lifting her to take him, then pressing her down against the sheets. She felt so good, so right, undulating beneath him. He possessed her with everything he had. When they came, it was together, hard and fast, and he surged into her, taut and deep.

She buried her face in his neck as the tremors subsided. Reveling in their closeness, he breathed in the sweet, womanly scent of her. And he knew. This…Amanda…was what had been missing in his life.

AMANDA CLUNG TO Justin, willing her heart to slow, her feelings to come back under control. The first she eventually managed. The second…well, she didn't think she would ever get past what had just happened. At least, not to the point where she could erase it from her memory. Which was why she had to put some distance between them. Now.

With a soft exhalation of regret, she untangled her body from the hard length of his and sat up. He lay on his side, watching with lazy satisfaction as she pulled on a robe. Amanda swallowed, not sure why she had fallen so hard and fast for Justin McCabe, just knowing that she had. And that her feelings, as intense as they were, might not be returned. That in his view, she might never be more than a conquest, or a woman he would like to bed and just be friends with. A notion, she knew, that could break her heart.

Finding her way back to sanity, she cleared her throat and regarded him with every ounce of common sense she possessed. "Well. As wonderful as this was…"

"You're kicking me out," he guessed, his voice rough.

She didn't want to. She also knew how easy it would be to forget all the reasons they'd never work out, and surrender her heart and soul to him. She couldn't let that happen. Couldn't stand to have her self-esteem crushed again. Because even if Justin didn't mean to hurt her, in the end, he would.

And if she'd barely recovered once—with a man she

had come to realize she'd never truly loved—she would not survive this.

Amanda shoved the hair from her face and twisted it into a loose knot at the nape of her neck as she paced. "It's no surprise that we made love tonight, or why."

He did a double take, but she forced the words out. "However, you have to know that we can't continue this."

He caught her wrist as she passed and drew her down to sit beside him on the bed. He looked like a male Adonis with the sheet drawn loosely to his waist. A slight smile curved his lips. "You're going to have to clue me in," he said with a bewildered shake of his head. "Because I thought we made love because we are incredibly attracted to each other."

Amanda averted her gaze from the muscular splendor of his bare chest. She resisted the urge to bury her fingers in the swirls of hair around his flat male nipples. "That was part of it."

His eyes lingering everywhere he had previously caressed, he took her hand and turned it palm-up. "What was the rest of it?"

Pushing aside the memory of the way he had just made love to her, not to mention the tingles still rippling through her body, she forged on, "You had a culinary emergency. I helped you out."

He held her open palm in his and traced her lifeline with the tip of his index finger. "It was lot more than just cooking together that propelled us into your bed."

Ignoring the need to join him there again, she met his gaze and didn't look away. "Listen to me, Justin." Deliberately, she tried again to talk sense into him. "When a man and a woman successfully entertain together, the way we did tonight, they can end up feeling like a couple even without an intense physical attraction for each other."

Tenderness filled his eyes. "And you know this because…?"

Sadly, Amanda admitted, "Because it's happened to me before."

He let her hand go. Continued watching. "With your ex-fiancé?"

Her throat dry, Amanda nodded. "His family owns a custom home-building business. They take on high-end clients, people who require wooing and entertaining."

Amanda sighed. "When Rob joined the business, he was expected to do that, too." She frowned, recalling, "He had one couple in particular he was trying to sign. The man and his wife were both incredible cooks, and they wanted a builder who shared their passion.

"I was putting in some custom carpentry on another home his family's company was building, and Rob knew I liked to cook so he came to me for advice." Amanda threw up her hands in dismay and shook her head. "One thing led to another, and the next thing I know I'm not just giving Rob advice on what to cook, but I'm in the kitchen with him…"

Aware Justin was listening intently, Amanda continued relaying her story. "Suffice it to say, the clients signed, and Rob was delighted. He took me out to dinner to celebrate his successful deal. We did a few more dinners." Her face flushed as she forced herself to go on so Justin would understand. "We ended up in bed. And we felt like such a great couple we became engaged."

Justin studied her, all empathetic male. "Which lasted until Rob found out about your background."

Amanda nodded, a mixture of pain and regret flowing through her once again. "Which is when it all fell apart." She drew a deep breath and stood. "The thing is, if I hadn't stepped into the role of Rob's helpmate, or partner or what ever you want to call it, we never would have ended up in bed together, just like you and I would never have ended up in bed together tonight."

Rising to his feet, Justin put his hands on her shoulders and waited until she looked him in the eye. "You're selling us short," he said with a look of sheer male annoyance.

Amanda tried not to think about how magnificent he was, with clothes and without. How incredibly, sexily masculine. "Don't you see? I can't romanticize what happened tonight the same way I did before."

"I don't think you're doing that. I think you're running from what just happened because you're scared that what we've got might have the potential to be something real. Or lasting," he said, taking her into his arms.

The hardness of his body pressed against hers, he dropped a kiss on her temple, another on her cheek, the corner of her mouth. He paused to give her a long, hot, openmouthed kiss that she couldn't help but return.

"And the way you're responding to me now proves it." He kissed her thoroughly.

Amanda knew she shouldn't give in to Justin again, shouldn't give in to this. But the moment he touched her, self-control vanished.

She let out a tremulous sigh. "Maybe just once more, to satisfy our curiosity about each other," she conceded.

"I'm all for making love again." He tumbled her back onto the sheets as if they had all the time in the world. Only, as it turned out, it wasn't once more. It was two more times. After which, Amanda was so replete and content she didn't have the will to toss him out. Instead, she spent the night clasped in his arms.

The next thing she knew, it was morning. Sunlight was slipping past the edges of the window blinds. She was alone in her bed. Sighing groggily, Amanda sat up and looked at the clock. To her amazement, the morning was half gone.

Not surprised that Justin had taken off, but happy he had been kind enough to let her sleep in, she stretched, got up and headed for the shower. She came out and had just gotten dressed when there was a rap on her door. Justin was standing there, compelling as ever. In deference to the intense heat of the July day, he was dressed in cargo shorts and a V-necked T-shirt.

"Hey there, sleepyhead."

His endearment sent a thrill coursing over her skin.

"Ready for some breakfast?"

Was she? And if they did eat together, would it lead to more lovemaking on the one day both of them could afford to take off?

"'Cause if you are…" Justin's voice was a sexy drawl.

Before Amanda could answer, she heard a vehicle coming up the lane toward the lodge.

They turned toward the sound. "Expecting someone?" Justin asked.

Amanda was about to say "no" when the white pickup truck came closer and she caught sight of the familiar green letters emblazoned on the side. "Actually," she bit her lip, "it's my grandfather."

A. B. JOHNSON WAS everything you'd expect a self-made man to be, and more. Justin figured the carpenter was in his late sixties. He was fit, strong, robust and nearly as tall as Justin.

A.B. got out of the truck bearing his name and company logo. He strode straight to Amanda, wrapping her in a bear hug. Blushing fiercely, she hugged him back. "Granddad! What are you doing here?"

"I came to see how you were holding up." The white-haired man released her and turned to Justin. "A. B. Johnson, here. Or Angus, if you prefer. And you must be...?"

Happy to meet the man who had played such an important part in Amanda's life, Justin extended a hand. "Justin McCabe."

Angus looked from one to the other. "Am I interrupting something?"

"Not at all," Justin replied cordially. "I just stopped by to invite Amanda to have breakfast with me at the lodge. I'd be honored if you could join us, too, sir."

Amanda gave Justin a look that reminded him that *she* hadn't said yes. Not that he figured there was ever any doubt, any more than there was really any doubt that she would make love with him again when the time was right.

A.B. smiled. "That'd be nice, thanks."

Justin ignored Amanda's obvious wish that he hadn't extended the invitation as the three of them walked toward the lodge. A.B. paused to greet all five of the dogs, who had been standing sentry on the porch. Tails wagging, each got petted in turn.

Inside the lodge, two places had been set, complete with floral centerpiece, on the long plank table.

Justin added another place setting and headed for the stove. "Hope you like pancakes," he said over his shoulder.

Her grandfather grinned. "I sure do."

Gesturing for them to have a seat, Justin poured three mugs of coffee, then set cream and sugar on the table.

Conversation quickly turned to carpentry. "How much do you have left to go?" A.B. asked.

Amanda slipped easily into business mode. "We're halfway done with all the carpentry. Then we'll have to stain and finish everything."

Justin didn't want to think about the time when Amanda would leave. He liked having her at the ranch.

A.B. turned to Justin. "My granddaughter making the grade?" he drawled, his faded eyes twinkling.

Realizing he and A.B. had something very important in common—a deep and abiding affection for Amanda—Justin smiled back. "By leaps and bounds, actually."

A.B.'s glance narrowed, considering. "You cook for all your help?"

Amanda cringed at the protective tone. "Granddad…"

Justin winked. "Just the special ones." He brought a platter of sausage patties out of the oven, and set that and a plate brimming with golden flapjacks on the table. He added butter and two kinds of syrup then went back to make some more.

"Although," Justin continued, pausing to bring out a pitcher of juice, "I did have an ulterior motive in asking Amanda to eat with me this morning."

COULD IT GET any worse? Amanda wondered, barely resisting the urge to duck for cover. First Granddad, arriving unexpectedly, obviously because he suspected that something was up with her. And now he was watching her every move, and Justin's, too!

"Really." Granddad sat back in his chair.

"I'm sure Justin just wanted to thank me for giving him a hand with the fund-raising dinner last night."

"What I really wanted to do," Justin clarified, with the gallantry for which the McCabe family was known throughout Texas, "was talk to you about the future."

Oh, no, Amanda thought with a sinking heart. *Please tell me he's not going to ask Granddad for permission to date me.* "Not necessary," she declared with an airy wave of her hand.

Justin just smiled and continued talking to her grandfather as if she hadn't objected. "Did Amanda tell you she'd been teaching carpentry to a teenage boy named Lamar Atkins?"

Granddad folded his arms across his chest. "She did."

Justin stacked the second batch of golden hotcakes on the plate and carried them to the table. "Good, 'cause I have to tell you that what's been going on here is nothing short of amazing."

Joining them at the table, Justin explained the circumstances that brought Lamar to the ranch and the attitude the delinquent teenager had when he arrived. "Everyone's impressed at the impact Amanda's been able to have on Lamar."

"Doesn't surprise me," her granddad declared, slicing into a crisp sausage patty. "My granddaughter has always had an enormous heart. Plus, a real talent for carpentry."

"To the point," Justin agreed, adding food to his plate, "that I'm hoping I can convince her to stay on, once she's done with the contracted work."

Amanda blinked. No way had she seen this coming! "In what capacity?" she asked.

Justin reached for the maple syrup. "Carpentry instructor."

"Hmm." Her grandfather scratched his ear thoughtfully.

Amanda didn't know what to think. She had not expected the two men to join forces. The only thing she did know was that, after having made love with him, it would be torture to work with Justin if they weren't going to become romantically involved.

And common sense told her that, over the long-term, they would not be.

"Thanks, but I already have a job," she said tersely.

Justin studied her as if looking for a way to bypass her opposition and change her mind.

Finished eating, Granddad pushed his plate away. "Despite the fact that helping people in need is always a good thing, my granddaughter's right not to rush into anything. There's a lot to consider. The overall stability of this situation, for instance."

Amanda relaxed in relief.

Justin rose, more determined than ever. "Want to have a look around?" he asked A.B. "See what I've been able to accomplish so far?"

The next thing Amanda knew, the three of them had piled into Justin's pickup. They drove the entire two-hundred-acre property. Went to see the neighboring ranch where the boys would learn to ride and care for horses under the tutelage of Dylan Reeves. Then they visited the park ranger station at Lake Laramie, where the boys would go once a week to assist in whatever way necessary. And finally they were back to the boys ranch, where they toured the bunkhouse, and then the lodge, and finally settled in Justin's office.

There, the talk turned to the problems and pitfalls of starting any new business from the ground up, whether it be for-profit or nonprofit. Before long, Justin was getting out his books. Her grandfather eagerly took a look, curious to see exactly how and where the boys ranch money was being spent.

Then, satisfied that Justin was an accomplished financial manager, A.B. offered to help Justin put together a financial prospectus on just what it would cost to set up an on-site workshop and offer carpentry instruction at the ranch for all the boys.

The talk grew even more detailed and intense as the two men bonded.

Confused and a little annoyed, although she couldn't exactly pinpoint why, Amanda eased out of the room. Given how pleasurably her morning with Justin had started, this was not the way she had expected her day to go.

"I HAVE THE feeling you're ticked off at me," Justin said that evening after her grandfather had headed back to San Angelo.

Well, he wasn't completely clueless. That was good to know.

"Why would I be ticked off at you?" she challenged sweetly.

His brow furrowed. "You tell me."

Her heart kicked up a notch. "Mmm, no." Amanda inched off her gloves and tucked them into the pockets on her knee-length overalls. "You go first."

Justin narrowed his eyes. "I think you're jealous that I spent most of the day with your granddad instead of you."

Amanda moved her safety goggles to the top of her head and swallowed against the sudden dryness in her throat. "You're partially right." She turned off the miter saw, unplugged it and walked out of the bunkhouse.

At seven o'clock the sun was inching toward the horizon. This time of summer, sunset was still an hour and a half away. Peace of mind seemed even more distant.

Justin shut the door behind them and came close enough for her to see the hint of evening beard lining his stubborn jaw. "Then suppose you tell me the rest of it."

Amanda struggled to maintain her composure in the face of all that masculine determination. "My grandfather has never approved of any guy who has shown an interest in me, including my ex-fiancé."

"Seems like A.B. might have had a reason, since your ex was obviously a jerk."

Amanda stiffened, hating it when he was right. "That's not the point."

He cocked a brow. "Then what is?"

She refused to be seduced by the satisfaction in his low voice. "Granddad likes you, Justin. A lot."

He didn't back off in the slightest. "I would think that would be a good thing."

"Well, it's not!" she scoffed. "I don't want the two of you being all buddy-buddy." *Especially under the circumstances.*

He stepped even closer, inundating her with his intoxicating scent. "Why not?"

Amanda put up a staying palm. "Because it makes things too complicated."

"In what way?" He caught her wrist and lifted it to his lips.

Skin tingling, she pulled away from him and walked to the edge of the bunkhouse porch. "In a way that leaves too many people getting hurt."

He went very still, his expression inscrutable as he waited for her to go on.

Knowing it had to be said, even if she didn't want to have to say it, Amanda continued, "Because, like I said last night, if I keep seeing you, this—whatever this is— will end badly."

He came several steps closer, his gaze roving her up-turned face. "It doesn't have to."

"Doesn't it?"

He shook his head, his expression sober, intent. "I'd never hurt you, Amanda."

Amanda only wished she were that naive. "I'm sure it eases your conscience to think so right now," she said. He was a McCabe, after all. And McCabe men did not hurt women.

But that didn't mean they would have a happily-ever-after ending, either. Especially with any real, long-term commitment between them out of the question.

Justin threaded his fingers through her hair, cupping her head with his hand. "Listen to me, Amanda. My conscience doesn't need easing where you're concerned, because I haven't done anything wrong. And for the record, I like your grandfather. He's a great guy. Very down-to-earth."

Aware they were veering into dangerous territory, Amanda said, "A.B. also knows something is going on between the two of us."

"I know that. I could tell that right away." He leaned closer still. "But even if I hadn't intuited that, I would have found out. Because after you left the office this afternoon, he asked me what my intentions are toward you."

Dismayed, but not really surprised, Amanda eased into a sitting position on the porch railing. "What did you say?"

Justin chuckled. "I said that I didn't know yet. That you were really kind of ornery and independent, and you liked to cook." He shook his head as if that were the worst complaint yet. "And what man could possibly want a woman in his life who knows how to turn burned filet of beef into the most delicious barbacoa enchiladas anyone has ever tasted?"

Amanda rolled her eyes. "Will you be serious?"

Justin gripped her wrist and tugged her to her feet. "I *am* being serious." He wrapped his arms around her waist and brought her snug against him.

"When A.B. mentioned that you didn't have an ideal background, I told him I already knew that, and it didn't matter to me…and it wouldn't matter to my family, either." He paused to make sure his words were sinking in. "Because McCabes know it's not the name that makes a person worth having. It's what's in a person's heart. And your heart, Amanda, is pure gold."

Chapter Seven

"Have you given any more thought to my proposal?" Justin asked Amanda on Monday, after Lamar had left for the day.

The truth was, she hadn't been able to think about anything else. The idea of staying on and helping create a program to teach kids like Lamar was incredibly enticing—even without the added bonus of working by Justin's side.

Amanda attached the slide for a cabinet drawer. "I'd be happy to help you design the program, but I can't sign on as a full-time instructor." *No matter how much a part of me would like to do so.*

He favored her with a sexy half smile. "Not even if your granddad thought it was a good idea for you?"

Amanda picked up the other slide and fastened it, too. "He wouldn't."

Justin didn't say anything for a moment. Then he took his cell phone out of his pocket, punched in a number and handed her the phone.

"Hi, honey."

Familial warmth spiraled through her as she set down her drill. "Granddad?"

"Justin thought it would help if I told you I want you to do this."

She glared at Justin, only to have him grin back at her

in a way that made her hormones surge. Pacing a short distance away, she continued talking to her grandfather. "I can't teach classes here. I have two jobs after this one, remember?"

"Not to worry," A.B. assured her. "I took care of it."

Amanda tensed. "What do you mean 'you took care of it'?"

"We'll discuss it next time I see you."

Amanda willed herself to hold her own with these two determined men. Shielding her face with her hand, Amanda avoided Justin's eyes. "Granddad, I know this is a good cause, but I have a responsibility to your business." One she took very seriously.

"Nothing trumps kids in need. Let me know if you and Justin require anything else from me." And just like that he ended the call.

Astounded, Amanda turned to Justin. "The two of you are ganging up on me!" Her heart took another little leap of anticipation as he neared.

A seductive tilt to his lips, he held her gaze in an increasingly intimate way. "I'm going to do what I have to do to make this situation work. So," he said finally, assuming—and rightly so—that she would help him in the end. "Do you have time to get started designing an apprenticeship program tonight?"

AN HOUR LATER Amanda had showered and changed into clean clothes. She met Justin in his office at the lodge, and though she'd braced herself for the prospect of spending another evening with him, nothing could have prepared her for the way he looked when she strolled in.

For starters, he had showered, too. Not a bad idea after a day spent running in and out of the Texas summer heat. He'd put on a pair of faded blue jeans, and an olive-green button-up. Shirttail out, sleeves rolled to just beneath the elbow, first couple of buttons undone, he looked relaxed. Sexy. And, to her secret disappointment, completely ready to get down to business.

Already behind his desk, he motioned for her to sit down.

"Your grandfather sent me a list of all the equipment we would need, as well as a list of prices and places where we could buy the brands he recommends."

Glad she had opted for a casual sleeveless turquoise blouse and a pair of ankle-length white denim slacks, she took the pages he handed her. The data was so well organized it didn't take long to glance through it. Amanda smiled. "This looks good. Which is no surprise. Granddad is as good with numbers as you are."

He rocked back in his chair. "I take it that isn't your forte."

Amanda sat back and tried to relax. "You've got that right. Which is why I've been dreading the day that Granddad asks me to take over the running of A.B. Johnson Carpentry."

He eyed her curiously. "Not interested?"

Amanda frowned and tried not to remember how good Justin's lips had felt moving over hers. They weren't going there again, she reminded herself. "It doesn't matter if I'm interested or not in handling the business side of things. Granddad spent his entire adult life building that company. The income the firm generates funds his retirement. I owe it to him to take over when the time is right."

Justin's eyes darkened protectively. "You should tell him how you feel."

Amanda shook her head. "I can't disappoint him like that. He's been too good to me. And who knows? Maybe by the time we actually get to that point, I'll find I *like* making out schedules, meeting payrolls and crunching the numbers."

Justin snickered, clearly not believing her for one second.

"Okay," Amanda conceded. "So maybe I won't love it, but I'll learn to like it."

A muscle worked in his jaw. "Sounds more likely."

Silence fell. Justin went back to looking at the numbers. A little bored, and a lot restless, Amanda glanced around. She saw a stack of folders fanned out on the edge of his desk. All had photos of teenage boys clipped to the front. She inclined her head. "Are these the first kids who have been chosen to live here?"

"No." Justin rose and went to the file cabinet. He brought out several more thick stacks of files and handed them to her. "These are the first two hundred candidates. Somehow, I have to figure out who is the most deserving and pick eight."

Amanda's heart sank as she flipped through the top dozen or so.

"Yeah." His eyes darkened. "I guess I didn't think about this part of running the ranch, either."

Her throat tightened. She looked through more photos. "All these kids need placement?"

Justin raked his hands through his hair and left them clasped on the back of his neck. "The hell of it is, I don't know where to begin, or even what criteria to use." He sat back down in his chair. "Should I take only kids from Laramie County when I know that some of the kids who are living in the inner city need safe haven, too? Should I select the kids who've been bounced in and out of different foster homes more times than they can count? Or someone who's never done anything to get in this situation—*except* have the misfortune to be orphaned? Or someone who has been in the system for practically their entire life and is desperate for a place to call home?"

Put that way, it did sound insurmountable. Amanda resisted the urge to comfort him physically. Instead, she sat primly in her chair, legs crossed at the knee, hands clasped on top of them. She was just a bystander here. "Mitzy can't help you?"

Justin shook his head. "She said it's really up to me, and/or the new director. What 'we' think on a gut level after reading the files. Because, from the social services department's perspective, they are all deserving candidates."

Amanda ruminated on that.

"On top of that," Justin continued in a low, husky voice, "I'm looking at the cost projections your grandfather sent me of what it would take to start up a bare-bones training program in carpentry, versus what it's going to take to get another bunkhouse or two built so we can bring in another eight to sixteen kids."

For the first time, she felt the weight he carried on his shoulders, understood the enormity of what he was trying to do. And respected his courage for having taken it on.

She rose, ready to offer much-needed solace. "You want to know what I think?"

He grinned at the hint of mischief in her eyes and stood, too. "Somehow I think you're going to tell me," he drawled.

She handed the stack of files back to him. "If you're going to dream, dream big—and go after it all. Use the vocational program to show what you're planning to do for these kids, and that in turn to convince people to donate and give the ranch the big monetary grants."

They locked eyes for a heart-stealing moment. "That was the plan."

Amanda put up her palm for a high five. "Time's

a-wastin', then." After they slapped palms she stepped back. "Let's get started writing up those skill lists and course descriptions." Once again, inexplicably, undeniably, they were a team.

AMANDA SPENT THE next few days working hard on the carpentry with Lamar at her side. Her evenings were spent with Justin, putting together a proposal for the board of directors. Included in their pitch was an innovative way to pay for the required equipment, insurance and instructor.

"Let's just hope the board goes for it." Justin monitored the pages coming out of the printer as they burned the midnight oil the evening before the presentation.

Amanda laid the folders side by side. "If the interest they all showed when they were touring the bunkhouse the other night is any indication, they will," she assured him with a smile.

Justin walked the first set over to her. Their fingers brushed as the proposal changed hands. "Thanks for agreeing to be the instructor."

She still wasn't quite sure how she'd gotten talked into it; she just knew she couldn't turn away from those kids in need. Not yet, anyway. Ignoring the sensation the brief contact generated, Amanda shrugged. "Part-time. For the first year or so," she reminded him. After that, they would have to see.

The second copy came out of the printer. "No one is going to be able to fill your shoes."

Amanda accepted it and continued assembling the material, one folder at a time. "Funny. That's what I expected my granddad to be saying right now about leaving his business." She caught her index finger on a sharp edge of paper. Amanda lifted her hand to her mouth. No blood, but it still stung.

"You know why he's not?" Justin continued. "He saw what everyone else did—how great you are with kids."

And you, Amanda thought. But not wanting to clue Justin in to her grandfather's matchmaking, she merely smiled and put her still-stinging fingertip to her mouth. "What time is the presentation to the board?"

"Seven tomorrow evening. Want to go together?"

As long as it wasn't a date. And it apparently wasn't. "Sure." Amanda paused. "What should I wear?"

He brought over the third and fourth sets of documents. "Whatever you're comfortable in."

She checked her throbbing fingertip. Actually, it was bleeding, just a little. "What are *you* going to wear?"

He set down the papers, left the office and came back with a first-aid kit. "Shirt and tie."

He opened the kit and took out a tube of ointment. Amanda's heart leaped as he came toward her. "Jacket?"

He took her finger, inspected it and dabbed some of the salve on her fingertip. To her relief, her finger stopped stinging right away.

"Probably not, given how hot it is."

She was thrumming with something akin to desire as he tended to her wound. She forced a laugh. "No kidding. Will July ever end?"

"I hope not." He put on a Band-Aid, followed by a kiss that seemed to say oh-what-I-could-do-to-you-if-I-had-a-chance. A thrill swept through her.

Aware just how little it would take to persuade her to make love with him on the office floor, Amanda recoiled breathlessly. "What was that for?"

"All the work you've put in." He bent his head and kissed her again, more deeply and erotically. "Because I couldn't have done this without you."

Amanda wanted to believe that. Just as she wanted to

believe they could make love one day, be friends the next and even work together for the next year without any repercussions.

But the womanly part of her, the part that had been devastated by her last breakup, knew otherwise. There was no doubt in her mind that a romantic liaison between them would be fraught with emotional peril.

Finger taken care of, she forced herself to go back to the task at hand. "Yes," she said over her shoulder, pretending his kisses hadn't affected her at all, when she was nothing but a puddle of need inside. Hot, melting, lusting need. Her back still to him, she drew in a bracing breath. "You would have done fine. Nothing gets in the way of a McCabe and his goal."

Lazily, Justin strolled back to the printer, which had stopped spitting out pages while he kissed her. "You see me as that determined?" His expression was inscrutable.

His easy calm was as maddening as her own welling desire. Amanda smiled. "And then some."

And not just when it came to the boys ranch, but to her, as well.

The question was, could she—would she—keep him a heart's length away?

THE NEXT EVENING Justin and Amanda drove into town together and went to the Lowell Foundation building. In a conference room next to Libby's office, the six board members listened intently while Justin and Amanda made their presentation.

When they had finished, they opened up the floor to questions. Mitzy went first. "So the cabinets and bookshelves you and the students make in the shop will be sold for profit?"

Justin expanded on that idea. "The money from that will

pay for the necessary materials, insurance and Amanda's time as instructor."

"Sounds great," Miss Mim said.

"I'm curious, though." Libby turned to Amanda. "You have no background in either teaching or philanthropy. So how did you become interested in tackling something like this?"

Amanda found the spotlight on her. "To be honest, I never even thought about it until I met Lamar Atkins. Looking at him was like looking at myself at that age. It really took me back."

"How so?" Wade McCabe probed.

Amanda gave Justin's father's question the consideration it deserved. "I know what it's like to grow up failing in every aspect of your life. If it hadn't been for my grandfather, if he hadn't helped me see that I could succeed at something, I don't know what would have happened to me. But the skills I learned from him gave me a way to feel good about myself as well as a way to support myself and provide a valuable service to others."

She paused to look all six board members in the eye. "I want to be able to do that for others. I want to help get the program up and running and make sure that you find someone able to step in when I leave to go back to my family's business, full-time, one year from now."

Mitzy jumped in, "Would you be amenable to staying on if we offered you a more substantial role in the boys ranch from the get-go?"

Amanda shot a look at Justin. He seemed just as caught off guard as she was. "What do you mean?"

Libby smiled. "We've all been talking since the dinner last Saturday. We all concur. We think you're the director we've been looking for."

"Ice cream," Amanda repeated to Justin, still in shock. "You want to take me for ice cream after what just happened in there?"

He grinned as if he hadn't just sustained a major disappointment. "My mom used to say troubles go down better with ice cream." He put a light hand on her spine and guided her toward the Dairy Barn down the street. "Might have been more of a woman thing, but we all liked to eat so we were on board, and darned if she wasn't right."

At the window, Amanda ordered strawberry ice cream with whipped cream and a sprinkling of nuts. Justin ordered the chocolate-toffee-vanilla crunch with extra candy on top.

Because all the tables were full of other couples, they took their sundaes down the street a bit to a bench along a deserted part of Main Street. Amanda had no idea where to start so she began with the basics. "Thanks for the ice cream."

He settled beside her. "Thanks for helping on the proposal and going with me tonight."

There were several inches between them, but she could still feel the warmth emanating from his thigh. She watched the people playing on the mini-putt course across the street. "I still can't believe they offered me your job."

His mouth crooked. "It wasn't my job."

She turned slightly to face him, her knee bumping his slightly in the process. "It's the one you wanted."

He dipped his head in acknowledgment. "Which is different from actually getting it."

This wasn't fair. Amanda faced forward once again. "I'm going to turn it down."

He caught her hand. "Please don't do that."

She looked him in the eye.

"I admit, when Libby first brought it up, I was a little ticked off."

"As well you should be!" Amanda burst out. His eyes darkened. "But the truth of the matter is, they were probably never going to give it to me anyway. I don't have what it takes to relate to kids in trouble the way someone like you—who's actually been there—does."

Amanda had never met anyone so selfless. "Lamar thinks the world of you now."

Justin sighed. "But he probably wouldn't, had you not been there to build a bridge between us." He released his hold on her and went back to eating his ice cream. "I admit, until now, I didn't understand what all the board members were talking about." He frowned. "I didn't see why intuitiveness and instinct were such an essential part of the director's job."

Justin turned back to her in all sincerity. "But having seen the miracle you worked with Lamar in just a few short weeks, I now realize we have to have someone at the top who the kids feel completely comfortable going to with their problems. Someone who is cheerful and energetic and charismatic. Someone who just 'gets it,' and has had the experience of turning her own life around." He entwined his fingers with hers. "That person, Amanda, is you."

Amanda was deeply touched by his faith in her, but she still had her doubts. "That part of the job I could probably handle. It's the rest of it, Justin. The thought of all the paperwork and the grant applications and meetings with big-time donors that overwhelms me."

He nodded in understanding. "First of all, I'm not going anywhere. I'll still be the chief financial officer, as well as the assistant ranch director. I'll handle as much of that as you want me to handle. All you'll have to do is delegate and then give the final signature. And you'll have time to teach the kids carpentry, too, on weekends or evenings when they're not in school."

It was still a big decision. "I'm going to have to think about it."

Again, he understood. "I figured as much. So why don't you take a couple days off, maybe go to San Angelo and see your granddad and talk to him. And then go from there."

AMANDA THOUGHT ABOUT calling Granddad and letting him know she was coming, but if she did that, he'd want to know why she was showing up in the middle of a work week and she didn't want to hash it all out over the phone. She wanted to see the look in his eyes when she laid it all out for him. She wanted to see his gut reaction. So she went back to the ranch, said goodbye to Justin and hit the road. Traffic was light that late in the evening, and she made it to her grandfather's home in San Angelo in a little over an hour.

As she expected, he was still up, watching a late-night comedy show. What she hadn't expected were the stacks of what appeared to be legal papers spread all over the dining room table.

Business evaluations. Several different purchase offers. A proposal for breaking down the business, and dissolving it. "Granddad, what's going on?"

"I'm thinking of selling the business."

"Why?"

"Because if I were to sell it now, along with the existing contracts for the local homebuilders and home-improvement stores, I could make enough to pay my expenses the rest of my life—and leave you a little something in the bargain."

Amanda sat down in shock. "I thought you wanted me to take over the business."

"Originally, I thought it *would* be the best way. Then, as time went on, I saw how uninterested you were in the financial side of the business. I realized it wouldn't be so much of a gift as a burden were I to turn it over to you."

No wonder he had been so enthusiastic about her taking a job at the boys ranch. "When were you going to tell me all this?"

"The next time you came home, or when the job you're working on now is done. Which brings me to my next question." Granddad paused. "Why are you home?"

Briefly, Amanda explained.

Granddad shook his head. "Fate works in mysterious ways, doesn't it?"

It certainly did.

Amanda studied him. "You really want me to take this job?"

"I want you to do what will make you happy," Granddad replied.

And strange as it was, when Amanda thought about happiness, Justin McCabe was the first thing that sprang to mind.

Chapter Eight

"Your granddad's selling the business?" Justin asked in disbelief when Amanda returned two days later.

Trying not to think how much she had missed him, Amanda said, "He's been fielding offers for a while now. He just didn't know how to tell me."

"How do you feel about that?"

"Honestly? Relieved." And strangely adrift, too. As if the future she had seen for herself—even if she hadn't really wanted it—was gone. But there was a lot that was positive in the situation. She had to remember that.

Aware that Justin was watching her closely, Amanda forced herself to continue bringing him up to speed. "With the deal Granddad decided to accept, he'll be all set, in terms of his retirement. His employees will be taken care of, too. The only things that will change will be the name of the company and they'll bring in a day-to-day manager. Plus, the new owner has agreed to place orders with the boys ranch carpentry shop once we get that up and running. So, in the end, it's all good."

Justin poured her a cup of coffee and watched as she stirred in generous amounts of cream and sugar. "I take it that 'we' means you've decided to accept the job?"

Amanda returned his smile. It would be so easy to get lost in his easygoing charm. In him. "With trepidation—"

and the fear I'll end up letting everyone down "—yes, I have."

"As I said before, I'll help you handle the paperwork end of things. I know initially it can be overwhelming."

Amanda widened her eyes. "Even for you?"

He sat down beside her. "When I came up with the idea to start the ranch, I thought it would be simple. I'd buy the land, and build a lodge, and start taking kids in. It turned out to be a lot more complicated than that."

She took a sip of the hot, delicious coffee. "How so?"

Ruefully, Justin admitted, "Well, even with the money I threw into the project, I was far short of what was needed." He went on to explain about fire codes, zoning regulations, building permits and other bits of red tape he'd had to cut along the way.

Amanda blinked. "Wow. I had no idea."

"Not to worry." He patted the back of her hand. "Most of this has already been done. I'll walk you through anything that's left, like the final series of inspections."

Warmth flowed through her as she studied the loving way his palm covered her hand. "I don't know how you manage to do all this."

Justin got up and went to the fridge. He came back with a chocolate bar. "Hey, the Alamo wasn't built in a day and neither was this. And we're further along than you think. Although, there are a few things that have to be done right away."

Amanda accepted the half he gave her. "Like what?"

"Tomorrow morning you have to go into town to go over your employment contract with the ranch attorney, Liz Cartwright-Anderson. The appointment is at nine o'clock."

Glad for the sugary pick-me-up, Amanda savored her share of the dark chocolate. "Will you be there, too?"

He smiled. "What would you prefer?"

"For you to accompany me." The words were out before she could prevent them. She had the feeling that with Justin by her side she would feel less overwhelmed. "That way, if there are any issues," Amanda continued, a little lamely, "although I'm not sure what those might be…then…"

"I'll be there, to help expedite the signing," Justin promised.

Nodding in relief, Amanda crumpled the wrapper in her hand.

"It's not a problem. I'll just call Lamar's foster parents and let them know we'll pick him up in town. He was supposed to spend the morning at the high school signing up for fall semester classes, anyway." Justin stood and took his empty mug over to the dishwasher. "So, are you ready to pick out your new quarters?"

Amanda followed suit. "What do you mean?" Once again, she felt three steps behind.

"Well, obviously, as director, you're going to have to reside in the lodge, same as me, so…why don't we go upstairs and have a look?"

Amanda had never been in the wing that housed the staff quarters. The only time she'd been upstairs at all was the day they had gone looking for the missing Lamar, and then only so far as the TV lounge.

A lot was changing, very quickly. She fell into step beside him. "Who else is going to live on the property?"

"Well, for right now, you and me. Eventually, when we get up to full capacity of 20 cabins and 160 kids, we will have other staff. A registered nurse, an academic or vocational advisor, and if we're really lucky, and are able to build a barn and acquire some horses, someone to run the stables."

"You're ambitious. I'll give you that."

"Yeah, well, if you're going to dream, dream big, right?"

When Amanda smiled up at him, a sizzling look of awareness zinged between them. The moment passed when he motioned for her to follow him. Justin led the way up the stairs, past the common rooms and the library to the door marked Staff Only. "There are five suites. I've got the one at the far end of the hall. Which one would you like?"

Amanda walked up and down the hall. The rooms were all the same and held a desk, queen bed, dresser, reading chair and ottoman. "You can add anything you like. Television, computer, stereo, rugs, curtains, whatever."

It was nice, but… "Can I put a kitchen in there?" Amanda joked.

"No, but you can use the one downstairs anytime you want, since we're planning to share the cooking and cleanup chores with the kids and the other staff, rather than hire someone to do just that."

"Makes sense." Amanda walked back to check out the rooms once more.

Justin was at her elbow. "Hard decision, isn't it?"

More than he knew. Should she choose the one next to his, or select one as far away as possible?

"Want to flip a coin?" he quipped.

Amanda shook her head. "I think I'll take the one closest to the main hall." *And farthest from you.*

He looked at her, his expression maddeningly inscrutable. Was he disappointed or relieved, she wondered?

He slid a hand beneath her elbow. "Want me to help you bring your things in?"

Her pulse quickening, Amanda moved on ahead of him. "Actually, I think I'd rather stay in the trailer for a few more days and not waste time on moving my belongings when we have so many other, more pressing tasks."

He gave her a long look. "Sure? I don't mind. It probably wouldn't take long."

Amanda's throat felt suddenly dry. Being so close to him was going to be an adjustment. "No, that's okay." She smiled briskly. "I'll get to it eventually." *Just not today.*

"OKAY, WE'VE GONE over the duties of the job, and the personal leave and time-off policies," attorney Liz Cartwright-Anderson said the following morning. She went down the list in front of her. "Which leads us to the fraternization among coworkers policy."

Liz's unexpected announcement sent Justin into a coughing fit. Several board members raised their brows. Amanda worked to contain a flush of embarrassment while Liz handed over papers to both Justin and Amanda. The three members of the board of directors in attendance already had their own copies, it seemed.

Liz continued matter-of-factly, "We had intended to go over this with you and Justin separately, but since you're both here today, we'll go ahead and do it jointly."

Which meant what, exactly? Amanda wondered, feeling even more embarrassed. The look on Justin's face said he was as surprised and uncomfortable with the discussion as she was. Working to maintain her composure, Amanda turned her attention back to Liz, who was still referring to the fine print on the contract in front of her. Liz read, "Dating a coworker is allowed, as long as disclosure is made to the board and a release is signed by both parties stating that both parties accept full responsibility for what does or does not happen within the bounds of said relationship."

"And if I were to choose not to disclose?" Amanda asked.

"Then that would be grounds for dismissal," Liz informed her.

Which would not be the end of the world for her, but it would devastate Justin, who had put his heart and soul into building the boys ranch. Amanda flushed. "Then I disclose that…um…Justin and I… Well, we aren't actually dating or anything…"

"But there is a spark," Miss Mim chimed in.

Amanda looked over at the retired former librarian. She nodded, affirming it to be so. Even though she and Justin had pretty much decided not to act on the chemistry again.

Libby smiled. "We all realized that the night of the party."

"But it didn't keep you from offering me the job," Amanda said in amazement.

Libby exchanged glances with the other two board members. "You're going to fall in love sometime, somewhere. So is Justin. And the fact is, you two do make a good team. You work well together, you treat each other with respect." She smiled amiably. "So, as long as your private life remains private, and doesn't affect your work, then the board has no problem with whatever may or may not be developing there."

"WELL, THAT WAS interesting," Amanda said half an hour later when all the papers were finally signed, and she and Justin had left the attorney's office.

"No kidding," Justin agreed. "I wish I could have forewarned you, but I didn't know it was coming."

Now that it was over, Amanda could chuckle. "I could tell that by your coughing fit."

He shook his head in comical lament and took her hand in his. "Well, at least we have the approval of the three ladies."

Feeling far too vulnerable for comfort, she pulled away. "The only problem is we're not dating, Justin."

He advanced on her, a sexy glint in his eyes. "Right."

He had a way of getting under her skin, like no other man. She turned to him in indignation. "We're not!"

He took her hand in his and lifted it to his lips. Lightly kissing the back of her knuckles, he teased, "So far."

Tingling from the seductive caress, Amanda disengaged her hand from his. Ignoring the racing of her heart, she stepped back and vowed, "It's not going to be an issue anyway. We have so much to do to get ready to open."

Justin glanced at his watch. "Speaking of which, we better get over to the high school to pick up Lamar so we can take him back to the ranch."

But Lamar was not in the school library, where registration was being held. Things went from bad to worse when his guidance counselor said she hadn't seen him at all. Amanda and Justin looked at each other. "His foster mom said she dropped him off this morning at eight, and that she watched him walk into the building," Amanda said.

The guidance counselor frowned. "Well, he must have walked right back out again, because if Lamar had been in this library I would have corralled him right away and signed him up for fall classes. And when you do see him, remind him that tomorrow is the last day for late registration for existing students."

"We will," Amanda promised. "So now what?" she asked Justin.

He held the lobby door for Amanda. "I'll call my brother Colt."

At the sheriff's department? Amanda faced Justin on the sidewalk under the portico at the front entrance of the high school. Funny, they weren't old enough to have a teenage child, but it sure felt like they were parents of the same wayward teen at the moment. "Won't Colt have to notify the court—which could lead to even more trouble for Lamar?"

Amanda knew the teenager had broken the rules, but she didn't want to see him end up in juvie, especially when he'd been doing so well all summer.

Justin placed a comforting hand on her shoulder. "We can trust Colt to do what's right for this situation. He may be a sheriff's deputy, but he's also the community liaison who runs the department's outreach program for troubled teens. That gives him some latitude. Not a lot, but enough."

WONDERING IF HE should have seen this coming, Justin searched the rest of the high school grounds. Amanda went over to Lamar's foster home to see if he had turned up there. And Deputy Colt McCabe went up and down Main Street, checking out all the businesses. They also scoped out the movie theater, the putt-putt course, the Dairy Barn and the bowling alley. Unfortunately, there had been no sign of Lamar anywhere when the three of them met up in the park at the center of town.

"He was supposed to work at the ranch this afternoon," Amanda fretted. It was close to noon.

Colt frowned. "He doesn't have a car or a driver's license, so he couldn't have driven there on his own."

Unless he had done so illegally, Justin thought, with a growing sense of unease.

Amanda sighed. "It's too far to walk." Her delicate brows knit together. "Do his foster parents own any bicycles?"

"There's one way to find out," Justin told her.

Fifteen minutes later, they knew what mode of transportation Lamar had selected. A blue ten-speed bike.

"I think we should head back out to the ranch," Amanda said to Justin.

He agreed and they walked back to his pickup truck

after promising Colt that they would keep him apprised of the situation.

"You okay?" Justin asked when Amanda hopped into the cab. He slid behind the steering wheel. She looked pale and upset. As if this might be too much for her to handle.

Her lips tight with worry, Amanda buckled her seat belt. "I'm just beginning to realize what a big responsibility this is."

A memory of a past failure assailed Justin. *This is not like what happened to Billy Scalia. It's just a momentary blip in the effort to save Lamar. She knows it. I know it, too.*

"You're up to it," he told her finally, determined as ever. "We both are."

To AMANDA AND Justin's mutual relief, the bike was parked next to the steps leading up to the front door of the lodge.

Lamar was out back with the dogs, drinking water from the hose. He looked hot and sweaty and immediately jumped to his feet when he saw them. "Where have you been? I was ready to work half an hour ago!"

"We were looking for you." Amanda put a hand to his face and winced at the heat of his skin. The poor boy was sunburned everywhere.

"I was supposed to be here," Lamar insisted.

Justin shook his head. "You were supposed to be at the high school, signing up for classes."

He unlocked the door to the lodge and the three of them went in. The blissful cool of air-conditioning hit them. With a light hand on Lamar's shoulder, Amanda guided him into the kitchen. She sat him on a stool at the work island and went to the pantry for a big jug of electrolyte drink.

Justin got down three tall glasses and filled them with ice.

Amanda rummaged around and brought out some salty pretzels, too. "So what happened?" she asked.

Lamar was clearly about to prevaricate, but he took another long look at their faces and his shoulders slumped. "I don't want to go back to that school, okay? It just… The thought of it… I can't do it. I can't go there again. That's all."

Which means something is going on. Amanda wrung out a clean dish towel with cool water and draped it over the back of Lamar's neck. "Are you being bullied?"

He made a face. "No. Of course not."

"Is it because you don't have any friends?"

Lamar scowled. "I'm not the rah-rah, join-a-club type. And everybody at Laramie High School does something extracurricular."

"It's a good way to meet people and make friends," Justin pointed out.

Lamar snorted and stuffed pretzels into his mouth. He followed it with a long, thirsty drink of Gatorade.

Figuring it was best to let that go for the moment, Amanda asked, "How long did it take you to get out here on the bike?"

"Three hours."

"It's thirty-two miles."

"I know that *now.*"

Alarmed, Amanda continued, "You could have gotten heatstroke."

"Yeah, well…"

Justin went off and returned a moment later with a can of sunburn cream. He handed it to Amanda. Wordlessly, Lamar covered his eyes and mouth and let her apply it. As the medicinal smell filled the kitchen, Amanda continued trying to get through to their young charge. "We were really worried about you, Lamar."

The teenager looked her in the eye, near tears. Whether

from sheer physical exhaustion or shame, Amanda couldn't tell. "I'm sorry," Lamar said thickly.

Justin stood, arms crossed. "Sorry's not going to cut it with the judge if it happens again."

Flushing, Lamar complained, "I was just trying to get to my community service work."

"You were running away from something you didn't want to face."

Like high school. Classes. Studying.

Lamar turned to Justin. "Can't I come here, instead of going to LHS during the day? Or keep working with Amanda, wherever she goes next, on more community service or something?"

Justin shook his head. "Amanda is going to be working here. She's been named the ranch director."

Lamar blinked, clearly surprised to find her the boss. "What does that make you?" he asked Justin.

As before, Justin took the demotion well, saying calmly, "Founder, CFO and assistant ranch director."

Amanda couldn't help but admire him. In his place, she wasn't sure she would have been so gracious.

"Well, between the two of you it seems like you're calling all the shots," Lamar pointed out. "Can't you *please* talk to Mitzy Martin? And get her to let me stay, even after my community service is up?"

HOURS LATER, JUSTIN stood in the doorway of the administrator's office and asked, "Not quite the way you would have expected your first day as director to go, was it?"

Amanda looked up from the stacks of papers on her desk. Just reading through the summaries Justin had prepared for her had taken the better part of an hour.

She dropped her pen, aware she'd never thought she would be a desk jockey, either. "At least Mitzy agreed with us that Lamar should be placed here as a student as soon as the ranch opens."

Justin took a seat in front of her desk. "We have our first kid selected, anyway."

Amanda smiled ruefully. "Only seven more to go."

His gaze trailed over her face and hair as sensually as a caress. "How about you take a break?"

Amanda threw down her pen. "You're right." She rose, massaging her aching lower back. "I should head over to the bunkhouse and get at least a *little* of the carpentry done today."

Justin stood, too. "That's not what I meant." He strode toward her, not stopping until he towered over her. "The carpentry can wait till tomorrow."

Amanda pushed aside the temptation to fall into his arms. She batted her lashes at him. "Says the person who isn't responsible for getting it done."

He stepped aside to let her by. "As your assistant, I'm responsible for everything you're tasked with and don't get done."

Amanda paused, wondering where she'd left her purse. "I'm beginning to like the way you think."

"Seriously, we should take the night off and do something fun."

Was he talking about a date? "Such as…?" Amanda asked, the search for her handbag temporarily forgotten.

Justin continued, "You've met Colt and my dad. I'd like you to meet the rest of my family. Three of my brothers who aren't normally in Laramie are here for my mom's birthday celebration. I'd like you to get to know them."

Amanda tensed. She'd been unwelcome before at family gatherings. She had no desire to be so again. "I don't want to intrude."

He reassured her with an easy glance. "Other people, friends of the family, will be there, too."

When that didn't help, Justin paused, took her hand in his. "It would mean a lot to me if you would go with me," he said quietly.

Put that way, how could she refuse?

Chapter Nine

Maybe she should have refused, Amanda thought an hour later as Justin drove toward his family's ranch in southeast Laramie County.

He sent her a teasing sidelong glance. "You can't be nervous."

Amanda reminded herself she had already met Justin's dad, and Wade McCabe had been very nice to her. "Should I be?"

He considered this as if it were a matter of great complexity. "Hmm."

"You're not helping!"

Justin chuckled. He drove past the gates of the ranch between the vehicles parked on the sides of the long, winding drive. He cut the ignition and turned to her, a devilish smile on his face. "Let's put it this way. McCabes stick together. So meeting them for the first time as a potential... ah...*significant new person*...can be a little like running the gauntlet."

Amanda rolled her eyes. "Now you're making me feel relaxed." And what was a significant new person by the way? Was that like a girlfriend? A special friend? Also known as a friend with benefits?

Mistaking the reason behind her unease, Justin reminded her, "Your granddad put *me* through the third degree."

Amanda pinched the bridge of her nose and briefly closed her eyes. She couldn't help but think everyone was jumping to conclusions a bit. It wasn't as if she and Justin had done anything more than spend one night together. They hadn't actually started dating. They hadn't made love again, although he had kissed her again. And now that they were working together, she wasn't sure they ever would take it any further. Especially since his relationship with the woman he had previously worked with hadn't ended all that well.

Aware he was waiting for her reaction, Amanda sighed. "Sorry about that."

"I'm not." Justin unlatched his safety belt, grabbed the present he had tucked behind the seat and came around to help her out of her side, as if it were a date. Or maybe he was just being polite, since he had obviously been raised as a true Texas gentleman. "It just means your granddad cares."

As they approached the big, beautiful ranch house, her heart was pounding. She swallowed and struggled against her nerves. Justin had told her not to bring a present; he'd said the one he'd gotten would be from them both, but was that the correct thing to do?

On the other hand, how could she have brought an appropriate present for a woman she had never met? A lady wildcatter, no less?

Amanda forced herself to relax. "So you're saying your family will be every bit as 'curious' about me as my granddad was about you," she said finally.

Justin slid a hand beneath her elbow. "In their own way, yeah."

She leaned into his comforting touch, inhaling the brisk

masculine scent of him. "What is their own way?" she asked, savoring the leather and sandalwood fragrance of his cologne.

Justin paused, then backed her over to the shade of a nearby tree. From the rear of the house, they could hear the sounds of voices, laughter and live music. "My mom and dad are both very outspoken when it comes to their opinions. But they are also very kind and respectful of others."

"That's good to know."

He gave her arm a comforting squeeze. "It's going to be okay. You'll see."

Moments later they were moving through the elegant, comfortable interior of the home, depositing the gift on the table with dozens of others and moving back through the kitchen, where a catering staff was busy. There, in the center of activity, was the "birthday gal" who looked about as far from the 60 sparkling on her jaunty crown as could be. Justin's mother was several inches shorter than the six-foot-tall Amanda. She was also lithe, dark-haired, bursting with energy and every bit as attractive as her husband and sons.

Justin encompassed her in a hug. "Happy birthday, Mom."

"Thank you. It's so wonderful to have you all here today." She embraced him again before stepping back. Extending her delicate hands to Amanda, she said, "I'm Josie."

"Amanda Johnson."

"The lovely carpenter everyone's been talking about." Looking absolutely delighted to have her there, Josie squeezed Amanda's hands warmly. "So, are you here as Justin's date?"

"No," she said, at the same time Justin said, "Yes."

Josie laughed. "Well, that answers my question!"

"We're friends," Amanda insisted, her face as hot as a prairie fire.

Josie's smile broadened. "Always a good start to any relationship." She plucked champagne flutes off a passing tray, handed one to each of them and clinked glass with theirs. "And exactly what I want for my birthday, too!"

Obviously knowing where *this* was going, Justin attempted to head Josie off. "I—we—brought a present, Mom."

"Yes, but you know what I want. What I *always* want," Josie teased.

Amanda waited to be illuminated.

Justin merely chuckled and shook his head.

"More grandkids, more weddings and more happily-ever-afters," Justin's dad cut in, as he came up to join them.

Amanda's face grew even hotter, but she kept her smile pasted in place.

"So you think about that tonight," Josie said, going on tiptoe to kiss her son's cheek. "Because I want all my sons to be as happy as their dad and I are."

"And speaking of our other sons…" Wade said with a broad smile, appearing to want the same thing as his wife. "The rest of your brothers are out back, waiting to say hello to you and Amanda."

Justin took Amanda's hand. "Then we won't disappoint. See you later, Mom and Dad."

Amanda and Justin moved off. It was all Amanda could do not to moan in dismay. "Your mom doesn't mince words, does she?"

Justin heaved a sigh. "Her heart wants what it wants. Which is all of her sons happily married with families of their own."

"How many have done that so far?"

"Two."

The back lawn was filled with people. White-coated chefs stood over commercial-sized grills. The air was scented with fragrant mesquite wood and barbecued beef and chicken.

His hand on her spine, Justin led her through the crowd, introducing her to guests and extended family. Finally, they found Justin's brother Colt. The sheriff's deputy had a lovely wife and a three-year-old son. An ancient Bernese mountain dog was by the child's side. The sight filled Amanda with an unexpected wish for a child of her own. *Justin's child...*

Next up was Justin's brother Rand—a big, strapping, macho-looking guy. Justin hugged his brother, who appeared to be there without a date. "Heard Mom's ticked off at you again."

"Yeah, well." Rand waved a hand. "What can you expect when you put a devoted environmentalist and a lady wildcatter in the same space?"

Derek, a venture capitalist based in Dallas, was as well-dressed as you might expect. He had an infant daughter cradled in his arms.

Justin's oldest brother Grady, a Fort Worth real estate developer, and his wife, Alexis, were supervising their little girl and several other small children on the backyard play set. Grady smiled at Amanda. "Colt said you're going to be starting a carpentry program at the boys ranch."

Amanda nodded. *Here's where it could get tricky.* "I am," she said, content to leave it at that.

Justin slid his arm around her waist, the proprietary nature of the gesture unmistakable. "She's also been named ranch director," he announced casually.

Grady turned back to Justin with a quizzical frown, clearly shocked. "Isn't that the job *you* were angling for?"

WORD OF AMANDA'S appointment spread like wildfire, and though Justin's parents offered their congratulations, Amanda could see that Josie had reservations about the unexpected turn of events. She wasn't surprised to see Justin and his mother take a moment alone a little later in the evening. He returned to her side ten minutes later, his expression tense. "Everything okay?" Amanda asked.

Justin merely looked at her. "Want to get out of here?"

"Won't your mom object?"

His lips tightened. "She'll know why we left."

They walked down the driveway. "Why do I have the feeling this has something to do with me?" Amanda asked uneasily.

Justin fished his keys from his pocket. "It doesn't."

"The director's job, then," Amanda persisted.

Hurt simmered just beneath the surface of Justin's expression. He opened the passenger door for her then propped one arm along the edge and rested his head against his taut biceps. His eyes searched hers. "Our family has a cabin cruiser out at the lake, if you want to go...."

Sensing he *really* needed to get away, Amanda replied, "Lake Laramie it is."

After ten o'clock, the area around the boat slips was peaceful, with only the occasional pocket of activity. Out on the lake, however, you could see boats here and there, their safety lights blinking.

Justin helped her onto the deck, undid the ropes and climbed aboard. Minutes later, they were cruising across the lake, the stars and half-moon nestled in the black-velvet sky, the warmth of a Texas summer night surrounding them. Justin drove the cabin cruiser until he found a deserted cove, well away from other boats. He cut the engine and dropped anchor, but left a few lights on deck, for safety, as well as the soft lights in the cabin below. For a while, they sat there in the semidarkness, accompanied only by the soft lapping of the water against the boat, the hum of cicadas on shore. The quiet was a blessing after the hubbub of the party.

Eventually, Justin went below and came back with a couple of long-necked beers. "You know, you don't have to talk about whatever-this-is if you don't want to," Amanda said.

He twisted off both caps. "I want you to hear it from me, not someone else."

This did not sound good.

He sighed, settling beside her on the bench seat next to the rail. "And if I don't tell you, you will hear it elsewhere."

Amanda took a sip of the cold, delicious beer. "Okay."

He opened up his wallet, removed a worn photo and handed it to her. It was a young kid with dark hair, olive skin and hauntingly-old-for-his-age eyes. The eyes of a person who had seen and experienced too much. "Who is this?"

Justin swallowed. "Billy Scalia. A kid I was trying to help back in Fort Worth, when I worked at the nonprofit there."

Their fingers brushed as Amanda returned the photo. "I take it the story did not have a good ending."

He ducked his head. "He died."

The pain and unjustness of that seemed to transfer from Justin to her. "Oh, Justin…" Amanda touched his arm.

Justin caught her hand and pressed it flat against his chest. "His older brother was in a gang and had gone to jail. Billy's mother was desperate to keep the same thing from happening to Billy, so she enrolled him in our after-school program. I was put in charge of coordinating services for him. I got him a grief counselor and a tutor, and signed him up for all sorts of sports and activities, anything to keep him busy and off the streets…out of that gang."

The heat of his body seeped into her palm. "But it didn't work," she guessed.

Frown lines bracketed Justin's sensual lips. "His brother's gang kept coming for Billy, wanting him to join. The peer pressure in that neighborhood is huge. His mother knew Billy wouldn't make it if he stayed, and she couldn't afford to get out on her own. I was working on a solution for both of them. She was even willing to put Billy in foster care for a while, if that kept him safe."

"But Billy didn't want that."

Justin let her go. He picked up his beer again, took another sip. "He didn't want to leave his mom, because then he felt the gang would blame her, and she wouldn't be safe." Justin stared out at the water. "Before I could get things worked out, the peer pressure got too much. Billy joined the gang on behalf of his brother and died during the initiation robbing a liquor store."

"I'm so sorry, Justin…." Amanda's eyes filled with tears.

He turned back to her, mouth grim. "That's why I left the nonprofit and decided to start the ranch, because I knew there were a lot of kids out there, some with parents who cared, some without, all needing a safe, quiet place to go, out of the inner cities. I wanted kids who lack the kind of positive nurturing background I grew up with to have that type of love and support in a residential setting."

Admiring his inherent gallantry more than ever, Amanda vowed, "And the Laramie Boys Ranch will be that."

Justin nodded in determination.

Knowing what he'd just told her was somehow connected to whatever words had been exchanged between Justin and his mother back at the ranch, Amanda guessed,

"Your mother liked the idea of the ranch." *How could she not?* "But she thinks you should be director. Not me."

Justin squinted. "It's worse than that."

Amanda traced the condensation on the bottle with her fingertip. "Tell me."

Another grimace. "She thinks, deep down, I'm afraid of failing another kid. That I let the director position go deliberately, and didn't fight for it as hard as I could have, because I'm already getting ready to quit the ranch—the way I quit the nonprofit and the big accounting company before that."

Wow. "Are you?"

Justin drained his beer and set it aside with a decisive thud. "No. The ranch is where I'm meant to be, Amanda." He paused, letting his words sink in, then stood and walked toward her. "I may not have the exact right background for it, but I'm a fast learner, and I'm going to do whatever it takes to make it a success."

"Even if that means ceding the director position to me."

He was only inches away, leaning over her. He met her gaze, his good humor returning. "That's not the sacrifice you may think it to be."

His sexy rumble sent a thrill soaring through her. "Really? How come?"

He smiled when she defiantly angled her chin and gazed into her eyes. "Because having you as my boss means I get to see you every day...and every night."

Amanda sucked in a breath. "And that's a plus?"

He sifted both hands through her hair, came nearer still. "Oh, yeah..."

His kiss spiked her pulse sky-high and weakened her knees. Amanda swayed against him, another thrill soaring through her. "If I thought it was just the sex..." she moaned between kisses.

"It's not." Justin deepened the angle and the sweetness of the caress and kissed her more passionately. "You know it's not…."

Amanda was beginning to see that.

Beginning to want to let herself go. Loving the way he challenged her, the way he wasn't afraid to take passion to the limit, Amanda slid her arms around his neck, pressed her body full against him and locked her mouth on his in a slow, sexy kiss that soon had both their hearts pounding. She felt the sandpapery rub of his beard and savored the exciting masculine taste of his mouth, the tantalizing tangle of his tongue with hers.

He made her feel so wanted. Needed. He was so big and strong, so unbelievably tender and patient in his pursuit of her. So good at getting her to live each moment to its fullest. To know that all that was wonderful was yet to come.

They descended the steps to the cabin and made their way to the double bed against the wall. He clasped her to him and she could feel the hard evidence of his desire. The heat. He kissed her so thoroughly it stole her breath. His hands slid beneath the hem of her blouse to caress her bare midriff. Sensation swept through her. Buttons were dispensed with one by one. On her shirt. Then his. "I want you," he whispered.

"And I want you," she gasped, her nipples budding beneath her bra. Lower still, dampness pooled.

And still he took his time relieving her of her skirt, her shoes. When she was clad only in a bra and bikini panties, he brought her to him. The air between them reverberated with excitement as he took in the swelling curves of her breasts spilling out of the lace, the jutting nipples visible beneath the thin fabric.

She spread her hands across his naked chest, exploring the silken skin and smooth muscle. The hardness and heat of his pecs. The width of his shoulders, his taut biceps. She nipped at his throat. "If we were to have a beauty contest, it's hard to tell who would win." She smiled against his skin.

He kissed the sensitive spot behind her ear. "You think?"

She let her gaze drop lower still, to the fullness hidden beneath faded denim. Her fingers eased beneath the waist of his jeans, finding his hot, hard length. "I do…" she observed playfully as her libido roared. "I've never seen a man with such an amazing physique." She kissed his chin, the underside of his jaw, his cheek. "And that face…" So ruggedly handsome. So male. So perfect in every way from the brilliant blue eyes to his rumpled chestnut hair.

He chuckled softly at the enticing ministrations of her hand, catching her lips with his in a long, sensual kiss. "That," he said as he unclasped her bra and eased it off, "is a compliment that can go both ways, woman of my dreams…"

With a wicked grin, he dropped the lacy garment to the floor and bent her backward over his arm. Tenderly, he kissed the slopes and valleys before settling on the exquisitely sensitized tips. Pleasure filled her with hot, mesmerizing waves. The last of her inhibitions fled. Wanting only to be his, she shuddered and let out a whimper of need.

Together, they shucked off his jeans and briefs. Her panties followed. Still kissing, they stretched out on the bed. At first facing each other. Then with Amanda on top, astride him. Hands on his shoulders, she kept him right where she wanted him, tempting him with kisses and caresses until he was as desperate to have her as she was to have him.

He flipped their positions.

His hands trapping hers, he moved lower, finding the silkiest, sleekest part of her in a slow, hot invitation. Amanda gasped, surging upward, and then there was no more waiting, no more playful foreplay. Eyes heavy-lidded and sensual, he moved over her and possessed her in a way that commemorated what they felt. In a way that promised even more satisfaction in the days and night ahead. In a way that said she was his. And he was hers. And for the moment, Amanda knew, that was more than enough.

Chapter Ten

Amanda accepted a cup of coffee from Justin. "You want to have a meeting every morning at eight?" She'd barely stepped out of her trailer when he was on the front porch of the lodge, waving her inside.

He favored her with a sexy smile. "I think it'll help keep us on track if I know what you have on your to-do list and you know what I have on mine. We'll add the rest of the staff as they're hired on, too."

"Okay," Amanda said, slipping off her tool belt and setting it on the floor.

He got out his list. "Do you want to move into this office or would you prefer to take the one next door?"

Amanda blinked, beginning to feel overwhelmed again. "Aren't they both the same size?"

"Yes." Justin nodded affably at his current office. "But this one is closest to the living area, the one next door is closest to the kitchen."

She grinned back. "Well, then it's settled, I'll take the one closest to the kitchen."

He looked into her eyes as tenderly as he had made love to her the night before. "So you want to move all the files over there?"

Deep breath. "How about we leave them with you for

now, since you know what most of them mean?" *And I'm not sure I ever will...*

Nodding, Justin moved on to the next item on his list. "The application for the big Lone Star United Foundation grant has to be signed and postmarked by Friday."

"That's the big one we're hoping to win?"

"Yes. Although there are several others that are due next week, and then another batch to start applying for right after that."

"So this grant application business..."

"Is a continuous process, since the deadlines occur all year long. But like I said, I'll fill them out as long as you want me to do so. All you have to do is read through them and sign them."

How hard could that be? "No problem."

"We have inspectors from the state social services department coming out tomorrow to do a preliminary inspection."

Amanda moved closer. "Why preliminary?"

"They want to have a look around and red-flag anything that will need correcting before the licensing inspection the last week of July."

She inhaled the masculine scent of him, wishing they were back in the bedroom instead of hanging out here discussing business. "Is it going to be a problem that the bunkhouse isn't finished?"

He inclined his head. "I doubt it, but they're going to need a firm date for when it *will* be done. And I would advise that to be at least a week before the final inspection, in case anything comes up on our end."

On more solid ground now, Amanda vowed, "I'll do an assessment when we're through here, and let you know."

His handsome features softened in relief. "Okay."

Without warning, the dogs jumped up and headed en masse for the front door.

Barking heralded a vehicle approaching the lodge. Justin went to the door. "Were you expecting a visitor this morning?"

"GRANDDAD!" AMANDA ENGULFED him in a big hug. "I didn't expect you this morning." How did he always know when she needed bolstering?

A.B. reached into his truck. "I have some papers for you to sign."

Amanda sighed at the sight of the legal documents. "Seems to be a thing lately." Briefly, she explained her visit to the attorney's office the day before.

They walked inside the lodge and settled in the living room area. "Well, if it were just you and me, I wouldn't require you to sign anything. But the new owner wants everyone who isn't moving over to the new company— which is basically just me and you—to sign a severance agreement with a noncompete clause."

Amanda looked over the contract, feeling unexpectedly nostalgic. "It says I can no longer work in San Angelo."

"But," A.B. pointed out cheerfully, "there's nothing preventing either of us from working in Laramie County. My attorney and I made sure of that."

Amanda signed where indicated. "What about the work left on the bunkhouse?"

Granddad pointed out an addendum. "I had everything here excluded from the sale, since it was the one project I had that was still ongoing. But, now that you've signed on as director…"

"It wouldn't be right for me to charge to finish up the bunkhouse, given that as of today I'll be drawing a salary for my work here."

A.B. smiled. "How is the bunkhouse going?"

Amanda leaped to her feet. "Want to come over and take a look?"

Together, they went through all she'd done. "You have what—three bedrooms and baths to go?"

"Plus the wide-plank oak floor," Amanda affirmed.

Granddad contemplated the stacks of flooring in the main living area. "How long do you have?"

Amanda shoved her hands in the pockets of her coveralls. "Less than two weeks to completion."

A.B. whistled. "And it's just you and Lamar?"

"When I have him, yeah."

Granddad understood why she felt overwhelmed. "Looks like you need some help."

Justin walked in to join them. "That we do," he said.

Amanda turned back to her grandfather. "The only problem is, you can't do this kind of heavy lifting anymore."

A.B. harrumphed. "That's not what Doc Parsons said. He said I can't do carpentry all day and then travel to and from a job. I can do one or the other just fine."

This was an old argument. "You promised Gran before she died that you would enjoy your retirement the way she never had a chance to before she became ill."

Granddad sighed. "You want the truth? It can get a little boring."

"I say let him help," Justin urged.

Lamar walked in, his backpack slung over one bony shoulder. He grinned. "The more, the merrier, isn't that what they always say?"

Amanda put the heel of her hand against her forehead. There was way too much testosterone in the room. "Y'all are ganging up on me, and it's not fair."

A.B. hooked an arm around her shoulder. "Relax, honey. It's all going to get done, and in record time. You'll see."

Before Amanda knew it, she'd been escorted to one of the bathrooms to begin installing the premade cabinetry with Lamar's help. Justin was tapped to carry the pieces of wood for the lockers and bookshelves to the cutting station set up in the dining area. He and her grandfather spent the morning measuring, cutting and sanding down the edges of all the required pieces. By noon, the necessary wood was stacked in each remaining bedroom. By evening, they had the storage units installed. The cabinets in the bathrooms were done. All that was left was the flooring.

"If the four of us work on it together, we could knock it out in two, three days max," A.B. said. "Then all that will be left is the staining and finishing."

Justin tilted his head respectfully at her granddad. "Helps to have another pro around."

Granddad smiled and slapped Justin on the back. "Helps to feel needed again."

A little irked to see her grandfather so chummy with a man she wasn't sure would be a permanent fixture in her life, Amanda retorted, "Well, be that as it may, you can't drive all the way back to San Angelo tonight, Granddad."

"Honey, I have to get the papers to the attorneys tomorrow. But I can come back the day after."

She could see how tired he was. "I don't want you driving home alone tonight."

Justin stepped in to help with the persuasion. "Why don't you bunk in one of the guest rooms tonight? Get a good night's sleep and then head home tomorrow morning."

"Please, Granddad," Amanda reiterated.

"All right," he relented. "If it will make you feel better, I will."

"THANKS FOR TALKING sense into Granddad," Amanda said several hours later. It was nearly midnight, but Justin was still elbow-deep in paperwork. She had been trying to get caught up, too.

He pushed away from his desk and leaned back in his chair. "No problem. Although I think you worry a little bit too much. A.B. may be seventy but he's in fine physical shape."

Amanda propped her hands on her hips. "Only because he hasn't been overdoing it."

Justin tilted his head, considering. "Is that your only objection?"

Amanda wandered closer. She stood facing him, with her hips propped against the desk, arms folded in front of her. "What other issue could I have?"

"I don't know." Narrowing his gaze, he studied her a long moment. "That's why I'm asking."

Amanda drew up to her full height. "I heard you talking to Granddad earlier today when we were working about the possibility of him working here."

Justin looked up at her, running his palm over the arm of his chair. "That's right. If he wants to work in the carpentry shop, teaching the kids the same way he taught you the trade, we'll put him on the payroll."

Amanda tensed despite herself. She met his level gaze. "I wish you had discussed that with me first."

Justin paused. "Are we talking about his health? Or something else?"

Up to now, the only one who could read her like a book had been Granddad. Trying not to make too much of Justin's ability to read her, too, Amanda said cautiously, "He was really happy to be here helping out."

Justin nodded. "And that's a problem because…?" he probed.

What if I don't work out and the board decides I'm not right for the job after all? What if none of this works out?

Would she and her grandfather both be set adrift, with no family business to fall back on? "It's too much of a commute for him," Amanda said finally. *Too much of a risk for me.*

And the key to her happiness, she had learned long ago, was to keep her life safe and simple.

Justin caught her hand in his, turned it so their fingers entwined. "So we'll set up accommodations for your grand-dad, whenever he is here, or find a place for him nearby. These are all details that can be worked out, Amanda."

She knew that.

Justin came closer. He touched her chin, angling her face up to his. "So what's the real problem?"

It was time to confide. "I'm feeling overwhelmed."

He released a long torturous breath. "Me, too." Amanda peered at him through lowered lashes. "You don't look overwhelmed," she pointed out.

He winced. "Paperwork, I can handle. A miter saw and nail gun—" he made a comical face "—not so much."

She waved off his anxiety. "Flooring is easy. Particularly if someone else is doing the measuring and cutting. All you have to do is line it up, drop it down and hit it with the hammer so it's nestled in tight."

He grinned confidently at her. "I imagine you'll help me until I get the hang of it."

Amanda grinned back. "I imagine I will."

Silence fell. Their smiles returned. Despite her hefty agenda, Amanda found herself relaxing.

Had her grandfather not been sleeping upstairs… But he was, she reminded herself sternly. So nothing of an amorous nature was happening tonight. Or would be on most nights, since they had to keep their private life out of the work realm.

Figuring this was good practice for the self-restraint that would be required of them in their new positions, she looked at her watch. "Well, it's late…" she said in a wistful tone.

He nodded, looking as if he were feeling, wanting, the same thing. Knowing, at least for that night, it wasn't going to happen.

Amanda cleared her throat, disengaged their fingers and moved away. "We probably should both get some shut-eye. The state inspector is going to be here at nine tomorrow morning." Since they couldn't make love tonight, maybe not tomorrow…or the day after, it would help to stay busy.

She would focus on that.

"WE SEE TWO problems that need to be addressed right away," the inspector told Amanda and Justin when he had finished the following day. "All the carpentry equipment and materials need to be secured when not in use, preferably in a building of some sort."

"Will a portable building work?" Justin asked.

The inspector nodded. "As long as there is a lock on it. Second, the travel trailer has to be removed from the property right away. The sooner the better." The inspector handed them their copy of his report. "Naturally, when I come back the last week of July, I'll expect to see the bunkhouse completely finished and ready for move-in."

When the inspector had gone, Justin turned to her. Obviously noting this was not good news to her, he pointed out matter-of-factly, "You were going to have to move into the lodge anyway."

Amanda walked back to the office that had been assigned to her. At the moment it contained a desk, chair and lamp, and little else. "I didn't think I would have to do that until the ranch opened." If then. She'd been hoping to wangle a way out of moving in, on some grounds or other. The truth was, she didn't want to be that physically close to Justin. Or get so emotionally entangled with him that she couldn't imagine a life without him.

Justin lounged against the desk, his knit shirt taut across his broad shoulders, looser over his abs. "Where do you usually park the trailer when you aren't living in it?"

"I'm always living in it. At least, I have been since I bought it a few years back."

He looked at her candidly. "You don't have an apartment or a house?"

She placed the report front and center on her desk and sank into her chair. "No. This is the only home I have. With the exception of my old room in my granddad's house. I mean, I can always go there, and I do from time to time. But the trailer is my home."

He studied her with an emotion she couldn't identify in his eyes. "A home you don't want to give up."

"Would you?"

He stepped closer. Reaching down, he drew her to her feet. "I sold my condo to live here."

Amanda flushed. "That was different. You bought the land and oversaw the building of the lodge and the bunkhouse. So this has to feel like your home now."

Justin drew her into his arms and slid a possessive hand down her spine. "It will feel like your home, too," he promised. Cupping her face in his hands, he kissed her with all the pent-up emotion of the day. Tempting her again and again, sweetly and evocatively, not stopping until she felt wanted beyond all reason.

Suddenly aware that things were moving way too fast, that if this continued she would feel even more confused and vulnerable, Amanda wriggled free of his embrace. "And that's another thing." Without her trailer home, without comfort and privacy… "We're not going to be able to do *this* anymore, either."

"Sure we will," Justin countered with a slow, sexy smile. "If we plan for it."

Talk about determination! She smiled as she studied him, suddenly feeling reinvigorated. "You really expect…?"

His eyes crinkled at the corners. "To keep making love to you? Yes, Amanda." He kissed the nape of her neck. "I do."

THE IRONY WAS not lost on Amanda as she hooked up her trailer to her pickup truck and drove it several miles down the highway to the campground Justin had assumed she wanted the first time they met.

Luckily for her, the Lost Pines Campground had a vacant slot at the far end of the park. There was no view of Lake Laramie where she was situated, but there was enough sunlight coming through the surrounding trees to power her solar panels. There was also an electric hookup in case her batteries ran low.

When she returned to the ranch around noon, she found a note from Justin on her desk saying that he and Lamar had gone to San Angelo to purchase a large shed and would not be back until much later.

"Well, fellas," Amanda told her five canine companions. "It looks like it is just us for the rest of the day."

Twenty minutes later she was proved wrong.

A gleaming yellow truck with license plates that said WILDCAT drove up. Josie McCabe got out, a huge beribboned gift basket in her hands. She smiled as Amanda and the dogs approached. "Is Justin here?"

Amanda explained where he had gone.

"Oh, dear. I had hoped to speak with him, and leave him this peace offering, before I left town again."

"You can wait," Amanda offered.

Josie shook her head. "Actually, I can't. But perhaps it's just as well you and I have a chance to talk privately, Amanda."

Able to see that a number of the items in the basket needed to be refrigerated, Amanda led the way inside the lodge. "It's okay, Mrs. McCabe. I understand why you would have been upset that I got the director job over Justin. It was an unexpected turn of events."

"But, according to both Justin and my husband, as well as the other board members, it's the right solution for what has been an ongoing problem."

That, Amanda thought, remained to be seen. "I've only been on the job a couple of days." And so far all she'd felt was overwhelmed.

"Which is plenty long enough for the situation to throw a monkey wrench into the relationship between you and my son."

Her hiring *had* made things awkward, at least at times. But how had Josie known that? "We don't have a relationship." At least, not an official one.

Josie set the fresh fruit on the counter. "He brought you to the party."

Amanda took the smoked meats and cheese and set them in the fridge. "He thought it was a good opportunity to introduce me to the rest of his family all at once."

Josie unpacked a box of cookies and another of cupcakes from the Sugar Love bakery. "Did he also tell you he hasn't brought a woman home since he ended his engagement to Pilar?"

Trying not to make too much of that, Amanda left the

cookies on the counter and put the cupcakes in the fridge. "Maybe he just thought it was time he got back in the saddle again." As soon as the words were out, she clapped a hand over her mouth. "I didn't mean for that to come out the way it sounded."

Josie laughed. "It's time for Justin to get back in the saddle and fall in love. For real, this time. I think you could be the one." A fretful look crossed her face. "I also think working together under such pressure could ruin things for you as a couple, and/or detrimentally affect the boys ranch."

Amanda had much the same fear but pushed it away. "It won't," she reassured Josie.

The older woman studied Amanda. "How can you be so sure?"

"Because," Amanda replied sagely, "I know what this dream means to Justin. I know how hard he's worked for it, how much he is willing to give up—" *including his pride* "—to see it become a reality. I won't get in the way of the success of the ranch. I'll quit before I see that happen."

JUSTIN CAME BACK around seven that evening. Amanda was in the bunkhouse staining cabinets a beautiful honey oak. "Need some help?" he asked, admiring her handiwork.

Amanda paused, not sure she wanted to feel any closer to him at the moment. And every time they labored together—at anything—they ended up feeling like more of a team. She gave him the skeptical once-over. "Careful. You could get this on your clothes."

He tugged on some plastic painting gloves and reached for an applicator. "I think it will be okay."

For a few minutes, they worked quietly side by side. "So how did your day go?" Amanda asked eventually.

"Good. It took some doing, but Lamar and I finally

found an aluminum storage shed with a floor that's big enough to hold all your gear plus a fair amount of wood. It's being delivered tomorrow morning."

Their forearms touched as they both reached for the paint tray at the same time. "That's great," Amanda said.

They finished one room and moved into the next. "I saw a gift basket on the kitchen counter with a card from my mom."

Amanda concentrated on the staining. "Yeah. She was here around noon. She wanted to make peace with you." An awkward silence fell. "She's sorry the two of you argued."

Justin snorted. "But probably not sorry for what she thinks."

"She has a right to her opinion."

Hurt glimmered in his eyes. "I wouldn't figure you'd be on her side in this."

Amanda shrugged. "That doesn't mean I agree with her." *Or think this could ruin our...whatever.* "I do think she has a right—as your mother—to worry about you."

"I'm a grown man. I can take care of myself," he bit out.

Amanda shot him a droll look. "I can see that." She waited until he met her eyes, then continued. "My point is, when I was growing up, I would have given anything if I'd had a mother who worried about whether or not I was doing the right thing."

His glance narrowed. "What did your mother worry about?"

Ruefully, Amanda admitted, "Whether or not I would interfere with her happiness."

"And your dad?"

"Worried about whether or not I would interfere with his happiness."

Compassion softened his handsome features. "That sucks."

Amanda refused to pretend otherwise. "Yes, it did. Fortunately, I eventually ended up with Granddad and Gran and they showed me the way families should be. You're lucky enough to have that, so…" *Don't look a gift horse in the mouth!*

He rubbed the back of his wrist beneath his chin. Squinted. "Hmm. Remind me of what my parents think about my life's work?"

Exasperated, Amanda replied, "You have a dad who thinks you're on the wrong path and a mother who thinks you *might* be on the right path but worries that if you stay the course, you could mess up your…" Oops. Damn. She hadn't meant to reveal that part of her talk with Josie.

"Mess up my what?" Justin demanded.

Amanda went back to painting. "Whatever this is with us."

He blinked. "She said that?"

Amanda drew a deep breath, expecting to inhale paint stain and instead getting a whiff of the soap and sunshine scent of his hair and skin. Still working, Amanda eased away. "Actually, I think she said our working together might throw a monkey wrench into our relationship."

Justin finished up the inside of a cabinet, without taking his eyes off her. "My mom called it a relationship?"

"Her word, not mine."

Justin's eyes gleamed mischievously. "I like that word."

With effort, Amanda continued to concentrate on her task. "Even if it's not apt?"

"Who says it's not?"

Amanda moved on to the next room. "You're digressing."

He picked up the paint tray. "I am."

Amanda settled before yet another cabinet. "And you are bringing the personal into the workplace."

Justin set the tray down. "Since the ranch isn't officially open yet and it's only the two of us, I don't think anyone else will mind."

She turned. "Justin…"

He stripped off one glove then the other, dropped them and took her by the shoulders.

"Just one kiss, Amanda." His lips hovered just above hers. "And then we'll get back to painting…."

"Staining," she corrected.

His eyes shuttered. "Whatever."

The next thing she knew, he was kissing her and she was kissing him back.

"So, what's the verdict?" he asked when he had finally lifted his head. "Is working together *helping* our relationship?"

Well, it certainly wasn't hurting it. Amanda lifted her lips to his for one more kiss. His head lowered, slowly, deliberately, and she said, "I think it just might be."

Chapter Eleven

It was midnight by the time they had finished. As Justin walked Amanda away from the bunkhouse toward the lodge he caught her hand in his. "You can't go back to the trailer tonight."

Amanda swung around toward him. It amazed her how much she wanted him, how much she *always* wanted him. The ferocity of her need put her off balance, and she pulled away from him but couldn't quite make herself disengage her fingers from the warmth and strength of his. "I'm tired."

He let go of her hand long enough to encircle her shoulders and pull her close. His lips brushed the top of her head. "Exactly."

His casual gesture felt profoundly intimate and conjured up an even deeper need for affection. Aware that it would take very little for her to go up in flame, and reveal just how deep her need for him went, she forced herself to create some distance between them. Then she flashed him an officious smile and said, "Seriously. I want a long, hot shower." *Preferably with you in it. But we can't have everything....*

He fought a smile. "We have that here, you know."

"I need clean clothes."

He let out a low laugh, his eyes dark with desire. "You can borrow some of mine."

Amanda quivered, thinking just how sexy it would be to sleep in one of his shirts and nothing else. Aware of just how close she was to surrendering to him, heart and soul, she lengthened her strides. "I also want a bed to sleep in." Reading the seductive direction of his thoughts, even as he fell slightly behind, she said over her shoulder, "My bed, not yours."

He caught up with her easily, and his gaze caressed her face. "Lucky you. We have a bed just for you right upstairs, down the hall from mine. In fact, we have an entire bedroom suite with your name on it. A bedroom, I might add, you are already supposed to be moved into."

Noticing her boot lace flapping, Amanda stopped at the front steps of the lodge, propped her leg on a step and bent to tie it. "I'm getting there," she replied irritably. Not sure why she was resisting the inevitable, just knowing that she was.

He paused beside her, his eyes roving her bare knee and calf with a lover's intent. "Not fast enough."

Another quiver ran through her. Aware her nipples were hard beneath the soft cotton fabric of her T-shirt, Amanda straightened. She ran a hand through her bangs, pushing them off her face. "You," she muttered with a beleaguered sigh, "are incredibly persistent."

His lips curved with a tenderness that she found even more distracting than his ardor. "And hungry," he allowed. He hooked his thumbs in the front belt loops of his jeans and rocked back on his heels. "Let's raid that gift basket my mother brought. She may not know how to cook for her five sons, but she does know how to feed us."

The culinary gifts had looked delectable. And, like it

or not, she was too tired to cook, and there were no open restaurants anywhere close.

Amanda gave in—on this. "Okay, I will make a deal with you. I'll shower here and borrow your clothes, but only because mine are so sweaty. And I will sit down to eat with you, but then I'm going to my trailer to sleep." Her look confirmed there would be nothing after that for either of them to regret.

He relented, eventually, shaking his head in admiration. "You drive a hard bargain."

"I do." Together, they walked inside, stopped to pet the dogs then headed up the stairs to his quarters. Not about to go anywhere near his bed, Amanda lingered in the doorway while he plucked a chambray shirt from the closet and a pair of gray cotton jersey workout shorts from the shelf. He stopped at his bureau. "Boxer briefs or commando?"

Amanda smiled, knowing how dangerous it would be to go there. "You will never know," she teased. "And neither, thanks."

His eyes glinted in return. "Soap? Shampoo? Towel?"

That was easy. "All of the above, please."

He produced the necessary items, and left her with the ease of a Texas gentleman, born and bred. "I'm going to shower, too. I'll meet you downstairs in ten."

Amanda called after him, "Make that fifteen."

AMANDA TOOK HER time in the shower, hoping the hot, invigorating spray would loosen the tightness of her body and the need throbbing through her. Instead, all it did was give her time to think about what it would be like to make love with Justin again, and to figure out if she could do so without falling hopelessly in love with him.

The answer? She wasn't sure. All she knew, as she got dressed in his shirt and shorts, gathered her dirty clothes and work boots, and walked barefoot down to his kitchen, was that she would never stop wanting him. Never stop relishing what they already had.

As she expected, he was waiting for her in the kitchen. He, too, was barefoot and wearing a pair of dark gray workout shorts that hit at midthigh and left his long, muscular legs open to her perusal. A white V-necked knit shirt nicely delineated his broad shoulders and flat abs. Crisp hair was sprinkled below his collarbone and on his limbs. She inhaled the soap and cologne scent of him and felt her mouth grow dry.

He handed her a tall glass of icy lemonade. He seemed to intuit that her emotions were in turmoil, even though his expression was casual. He brought the platter of hickory-smoked meats and cheeses to the table, and added a loaf of hearty sourdough bread and some spicy mustard from the fridge. "You'll be happy to know I texted my mom."

Amanda watched him open jars of olives, pickles and jalapeño peppers. She thought about the conversation they'd had earlier—one that had seemed to go nowhere at the time. "What did you say?"

Grinning, he brought down two plates. "'Thanks for the peace offering. Amanda likes you a lot even when you're wrong.'"

Amanda laughed ruefully. She added napkins and silverware then sat beside him at the kitchen island. She propped her chin on her hand and studied him. Although not yet dry, his hair was rumpled and very touchable. "You always have to have the last word, don't you?"

He turned on his stool so he was facing her. He tugged at a lock of her still-damp hair. "Pretty much." His husky voice sent shivers down her spine.

Amanda swallowed. "Did she text you back?"

His gorgeous blue eyes crinkled at the corners. "Yep."

Their eyes met, held. "What did she say?"

"'I love you.'"

The sober words hung between them. "That's it?"

He nodded. Another poignant silence fell. "I'll give her this," Amanda said, feeling a hint of moisture gather behind her eyes. "Your mom knows how to put an end to an argument."

Justin nodded, looking touched, too. "That she does."

Talk turned to the ranch, and all that had yet to be done, as they made sandwiches and savored each bite. They finished off their late-night snack with German chocolate cupcakes from the Sugar Love bakery. Replete, they rose to put the leftovers away and do their dishes. In a corner of the kitchen, the five mutts watched them with sleepy eyes.

Amanda walked over to give them their post-meal tidbits. Finished, she patted each one on the head. "The dogs are tired."

Justin nodded. "They're wondering why *we* aren't asleep."

Amanda realized there was still so much she wanted to know about Justin. She sauntered back to him, acutely aware of what she was wearing and what she was not. If she weren't so worried about having her heart broken again, they would have headed straight to bed. Working to keep it casual, she sat down to put on her boots, without socks this time. "What's your normal bedtime?"

His eyes gleamed wickedly. "Depends on what I'm doing."

Best not go there. She sent him a casual look over her shoulder. "Quit dodging the question." They needed to get back on non-innuendo-laced turf.

"On a normal work night, I am usually in bed by eleven. Weekends can be later." He paused, expression deadpan.

"Lately, there have been nights when I've hardly had any sleep at all."

She chuckled despite herself. "Got to watch that. Some habits can be hard to break," she warned with mock solemnity.

He came toward her. Taking her hand as if he were a knight assisting a princess, he drew her to her feet. His hands circled her waist, bringing her closer so her breasts grazed his chest. "There are some habits I don't want to break."

How well she understood that, Amanda thought, as an aura of pent-up longing surrounded them.

Tingling, aware she should have put her bra back on whether it was sweaty or not, she withdrew her hand from his and took a step back. "Well. Thanks for the meal."

He held her eyes, a lot more intimately. "Thanks for keeping me company."

Her yearning multiplied. She struggled, then calling on every bit of self-control she possessed, found her resolve. "But I better go."

He touched her arm. "I'll escort you."

Amanda slipped away from him, grabbing her bundle of dirty clothing and her purse. She held them in front of her like a shield. "Thanks for the offer, but that's really not necessary."

He leaned down and touched his lips to her temple, clearly aware she was using politeness as a shield. "Exactly why I'm doing it."

Amanda thought about arguing but decided that it would delay the inevitable.

She got in her pickup truck. Justin got in his.

It only took five minutes to reach the campground and drive through the rows and rows of trailers until they reached hers. They both parked their vehicles.

The grounds were quiet and mostly dark.

He followed her to her door. She looked at the handsome contours of his face and felt a tremor go through her. "I really am not inviting you in," she whispered.

He stepped closer and she forgot to breathe.

"A good-night kiss here will do just fine." Her heart racing, Amanda lifted her hands to his shoulders. Their lips met. And once the kiss started it seemed impossible to stop, even more impossible to control. She groaned. "You really are testing my willpower."

He brushed his thumb across her cheek. "And you're testing mine."

"Justin…"

Aching with need, she pressed her face into his shoulder. Her heart and body sent conflicting signals to her brain. Her body won.

She let out a heartfelt sigh, lifted her head and looked into his mesmerizing blue eyes. She could pretend all she wanted. Deny it all she wanted. But the truth was, she wanted to take it to the next level with him. Wanted…well, she wasn't sure what she wanted, except him. And that wasn't going to change. She splayed her hands across his chest, felt the rapid thud of his heart and slid them lower. She itched to undress him. To…

Amanda caught her breath, then whispered, "I'm thinking you better come in before we give the other campers a show."

His voice caressed her as surely as his eyes. He bent to kiss her temple. "I'm thinking the exact same thing."

AMANDA DIDN'T KNOW what it was about Justin, but the minute they were alone together she started to glow from the inside out.

She took his hand and led him to the bed, sliding her

fingers beneath the hem of his T-shirt and tugging it up and over his head. She dropped it onto the floor. "Anyone ever tell you that you are so darn irresistible it's mind-boggling?"

He started at the bottom of her shirt and unbuttoned his way up. A second later, it, too, was coming off. Slowly—over her shoulders, down her arms.

His hands skimmed across her ribs and upward. "Did I ever tell you that you have the most beautiful breasts?" His smile was slow and sure, and so hot it could have started a fire.

He bent to kiss a nipple. Her eyes closed as he stroked and suckled. A shiver racked her body and she couldn't catch her breath. She opened her eyes then impatiently reached for the waistband on his shorts. "Everything about you is beautiful, too."

The flatness of his abs, the smoothness of his skin, the sheer masculinity of his hips and lower abs, and…that, too…

Amanda laughed in surprise. "You're…"

"Commando. Mmm-hmm." Clearly aroused, he caught her against him, found the waistband of her borrowed shorts and eased them down. "And what do you know," he chuckled as the shorts hit the floor. "You're commando, too."

"Commando with boots." She glanced at her feet.

He slipped off his moccasin-style leather loafers and bent down to untie her laces.

"Naked is better."

"It certainly is."

The next thing she knew, her boots were off. Still kneeling, he hauled her in tight against him, parting her thighs and giving her a kiss that was long and wet and deep. Her hands were in his hair as he proved he knew her body better than she did. A whimper escaped her throat. Then, suddenly, she was catapulting over the edge, a quivering tangle of sensation. "I want more," she whispered, urging him up.

He joined her on the bed. "We'll have more," he said, his voice husky with promise. He caught her against him, his mouth meeting hers in perfect harmony. The kiss was slow and romantic. Rough and heartfelt. Tender and easy.

He was claiming her completely in the most primal way she had ever allowed, and she reveled in the heat of his body, the proof of his desire. The shocking extent of his need for her, too.

She relished the tenderness, the knowledge that something about this, the way they couldn't help but come together, had opened up her heart. Made her want to want and need him, the way she had never wanted or needed anyone before.

JUSTIN KNEW, MUCH as Amanda pretended otherwise, that there were still barriers between them. The fact that she didn't think she was good enough for anyone worthwhile. The fact she liked to keep one foot, if not her whole body, out the door. The fact that she didn't want to think about anything more than the moment she was in.

In the past, he'd felt the same way.

Now, things were different.

Now he wanted her with him, pressing her warm curvy body into his until neither of them could think. He wanted her soft, silky hands sliding all over him. Just as they were now. He wanted her on top of him, kissing him madly, and then beneath him, surrendering softly.

He wanted her open and wet and willing, moaning and wrapping her legs around his waist. He wanted to go deep inside her and feel her clench around him. And even when she did that, her hips rocking up against his, he couldn't get enough.

He met her eyes as they began to move in tandem.

Harder, faster…slower, deeper.

Until they were both sighing and panting for more.

And they gave it. One to the other, wildly, passionately, until at last there was no more holding back, no more seeking the best connection yet. They were soaring, pinnacling, the thundering ache in his body replaced by the shimmering satisfaction they gave each other, and the lingering yearning in his heart.

JUSTIN FELL ASLEEP with Amanda wrapped in his arms. He awakened as the first light of dawn was slipping in through the windows. Easing away from her, he rose from the bed and began to dress.

Amanda slept on, looking like an angel. With regret, he went in search of his wallet and keys. They were on the table at the front of the trailer, next to an application for a long-term lease for a space at the Lost Pines Campground.

Amanda's writing was all over it.

He was still staring at it when she came up behind him. Wrapped in a robe, she slid her arms around his waist and laid her head against his shoulder. He turned slightly, so he could put his arms around her.

She looked up at him, frowned as if perplexed. "Is something wrong?" Her voice was soft.

Ask her. "Are you thinking about keeping the trailer here indefinitely?" he asked finally. When she had personal quarters back at the ranch and him just waiting for her to move all the way in? What did this mean?

Her eyes giving nothing away, Amanda lifted her shoulders. "Well, I have to park it somewhere, since I can't keep it at the ranch anymore. It makes sense for it to be nearby."

There was certainly one reason he would not only understand but applaud that decision. Justin scrutinized her closely. "So we'll have a place to be alone besides a hotel room or my family's houseboat?"

Amanda hesitated, running a hand through her tousled blond hair. "Well, sure," she said finally.

Justin tensed. So that wasn't it.

"I just feel better if my home is nearby," Amanda said finally. "Even if, technically, it's going to be a home away from home, once the ranch opens and the kids start arriving."

Justin guessed he could understand that. Especially since the trailer was the closest thing she had to a home of her own.

He pushed his worries aside. They had time to work all this out. Meanwhile, with everything they had on their agendas, they couldn't afford to get bogged down in minutiae. "I've got to get back to the ranch and take care of the dogs."

Reluctantly, she led him toward the door. "I'll see you later, then."

Later, Justin thought with a twinge of disappointment, as he kissed her again and headed out.

When all he really wanted was the here and now. And the promise that, at the end of the day, she wouldn't decide their love affair was too complicated and slip out of his life as swiftly and unexpectedly as she had come in.

Chapter Twelve

An hour later, Amanda was in the office. Justin stood beside her desk, multiple stacks of papers in hand. "The first is the application for the state licensing board. The second and third are both small-grant applications. They're all ready to go. They just need to be signed and mailed."

Acutely aware of how good he looked in his beige knit shirt, casual green cargoes and work boots, Amanda accepted the files he handed her. "I can handle that."

His tall frame radiating barely leashed energy, he waited until she had set them aside before continuing. "You're going to need to read through them first, though, so that you're familiar with all the information and to make sure all is as it should be."

Amanda hated paperwork, but she also knew this was part of being ranch director. She was going to have to learn to like it. She put the folders back, front and center on her desk and flashed a smile. "No problem."

Justin reached for another folder. "We've received notice from the state that we're being audited."

Her heart sank as she saw the letter containing the list of all the items the state wanted to review.

Picking up on her panic, Justin curved a reassuring hand over her shoulder. "It's no big deal," he said, giving her a brief, comforting squeeze. "We have to do this periodically to maintain our nonprofit status. As CFO, I'll handle that."

Thank goodness. Amanda would not have known where to begin.

He removed his hand and continued down his list. "You saw the email this morning from Mitzy?"

Amanda had just read it when he walked in. "About Lamar." It was part good news, part bad.

Justin nodded, looking as concerned as she felt. "You want to tell him of social services' decision when he comes in?"

Amanda replied, "I'd like us to do it together, if it's okay with you." She lifted her eyes to his and felt a tiny thrill sweep through her when their gazes meshed.

"Sounds good." Apparently a lot better at keeping his emotions out of the workplace than she was, Justin sorted through his notes with laudable efficiency. "There was also a request for phone interviews from the local paper. They want to get your feelings about being named director of the ranch before they go to press this afternoon."

An interview? Already? Heaven help her. She felt so overwhelmed she could barely breathe. "What do I say?"

"Whatever you want. Although I have to warn you. I know that reporter. She's always looking for the sensational side of every issue, to jazz up her copy. She'll probably ask you how you feel about beating me out of a job everyone knew that I wanted." Justin paused. "She asked me."

"What did you say?"

"That I agree you have that something special the board has been looking for all along, and you'll do a tremendous job here."

Amanda caught her breath. "You really mean that?"

Nodding, he locked eyes with her, his expression every

bit as tender and giving as when they made love. "I do," he said softly.

Talk about gallantry. Justin was a bighearted Texan, through and through. The kind of man she had always dreamed about but never believed truly existed, until now.

"And don't forget the TV news producer from KTLZ is coming out to do the advance work on the segment about the ranch later today."

Amanda made note of that on her own incredibly long to-do list.

"I'm still working on the big grant application." He pointed to the stack of at least one hundred pages, if not more, on his desk. "That's due at the end of next week."

Amanda blinked at the enormity of the application. "That's it?"

"What I've compiled so far," Justin allowed. "There's still a ways to go."

Feeling like she would perish if she had to sit, trapped, behind that desk one second longer, Amanda rose and paced toward the window. She looked out at the lawn, saw the bunkhouse, which still needed a lot of work.

Justin put down his folders and came toward her. He stood behind her and massaged her shoulders. "It's okay. I've got it," he reassured.

Amanda trembled. "But should you have to?" she couldn't help but ask.

She pivoted toward him, her arm grazing the hard musculature of his chest. "I'm beginning to feel like I'm all hat and no cattle—not only full of it for even taking this job, but completely incompetent!"

One corner of his mouth quirked up at her self-effacing description. "Stop being so hard on yourself. You'll feel differently about everything once everything is set up and the counselors and kids start arriving. When you have seven other boys to help acclimate and mentor, you'll not only be completely in your element, you'll know why the board wanted you as director."

Amanda didn't doubt she would be able to do a good job mentoring the boys, and looked forward to setting up the carpentry shop and teaching woodworking. But as for the rest of it, the business matters she was inundated with now—or rather simply signing off on—how much of that would she ever actually be capable of doing?

She met his tender, reassuring gaze. "It still seems unfair, Justin. I'm the ranch director. Yet you're still doing all the administrative work."

"You'll transition into a lot of it as time goes on. Although, to be honest, I imagine we'll both continue doing double and triple duty until we get fully staffed. There's simply no other way to get everything accomplished."

"That's true." She leaned her head on his chest, absorbing his warmth and strength.

He stroked a hand down her spine. "The most important thing is getting the kids settled. And speaking of wayward teens…" Justin smiled as a car door slammed outside.

A minute later, Lamar walked in.

Justin and Amanda met Lamar in the living room. Figuring it would be more comfortable than her office, Amanda motioned for the teen to sit on the sofa. She and Justin pulled up chairs on the other side of the coffee table. "Social services has decided you will be our first residential student," Amanda informed him, watching as Lamar beamed with delight. "On one condition." Amanda paused. "You have to agree to attend Laramie High School in the fall. And you have to be serious about it. No more skipping classes."

Resentment surfaced, as expected. "I told you both. I hate it there."

"Doesn't matter." Justin backed Amanda up firmly. "This is nonnegotiable."

Amanda handed Lamar the course catalogue. "To reserve your slot in the first bunkhouse, you have to sign up for classes at LHS today."

Lamar slouched in his chair, all belligerent teen. He thumbed through the catalog listlessly, then shoved it back toward Amanda. "You decide."

Amanda figured that was as far as Lamar was willing to go when it came to cooperation. She picked up a pen, wrote his name and grade across the top of the form, and looked at the instructions the guidance counselor had sent along with the course list. "Okay. Well, first, you have to sign up for Remedial Math and Remedial Language Arts/English, to get you caught up on the requirements. You also have to take World History and Physical Science over again, too, since you flunked both of those last year."

Lamar scowled and started to rise. "Whatever you say."

Amanda shook her head and motioned for him to sit back down. "You're not done yet. You have two more slots left. One can be Physical Education."

Lamar groaned. He put his hands on either side of his head in a demonstration of abject misery. "I hate P.E."

"Everyone does, except the jocks," Justin sympathized. "But it's required. And it doesn't involve studying."

Lamar harrumphed. "Ha! I wish! The coach gives written tests on the rules of each sport."

Justin was briefly taken aback. "Then we'll find a creative way to help you learn the rules, either through practice or watching games on TV, which even you have to admit that you like."

Amanda understood what it was to hate the academic classroom and feel as though you just didn't belong in the traditional school environment. "There is a woodworking class for an elective." She glanced over the description. "Basically, you learn the fundamentals."

Lamar rolled his eyes. "I already know them."

"Which should make it easy for you to excel. And maybe even help some of the other kids who are struggling."

Her attempt to look on the bright side failed. The silence grew even more tense. Finally, Lamar shoved his hands through his hair. "I really have to go to LHS?" he asked miserably. "Again?"

Amanda wished she could tell him there was another option, but social services was not currently offering studying for the GED exam as an alternative path for a habitual truant. With a sigh, she nodded. "If you want to stay here on the ranch, yes, you have to attend the local high school.

"We'll make sure you get the extra help you need to get caught up," Justin reassured the boy. "Even if it means hiring tutors."

Lamar looked even more distraught. For a long moment, he seemed to want to say something. Finally, he stared glumly at Amanda and lifted a shoulder. "Fine. Can I go to work on the bunkhouse now?"

Amanda nodded. "I'll be right with you."

Lamar dashed out of the lodge. The dogs greeted him on the porch. Apparently needing the solace they offered, he knelt to pat them.

Justin and Amanda walked into the office to fax the forms over to the high school guidance office. "Congratulations on getting him signed up for classes," Justin said, preparing a copy for Mitzy and social services, too.

Amanda hadn't done it alone; they both knew that. She punched in the number on the machine. "I just wish he were happier about it."

Justin gave her a commiserating glance. "At the moment, I think this is the most we can expect."

Amanda knew that, too. She just wished she felt happier about *that*.

Luckily, for all their sakes, Lamar's mood improved dramatically as soon as they started working on the bunkhouse. It lifted even more when Granddad arrived to take over, while Justin and Amanda led the KTLZ producer on a tour of the facilities.

The fortysomething brunette was blunt-spoken and energetic. "I think the two of you are everything we're looking for in our Local Heroes series. Helping kids is going to resonate with viewers of all ages. And, of course, it doesn't hurt that we've got a picturesque ranch setting with two beautiful young people—the local golden boy and the former bad girl—joining forces to lead the program."

Amanda flushed self-consciously. She knew it was part of her appeal and the reason she'd been asked to lead the boys ranch, but she hated being known as a former delinquent. It was just so embarrassing when she was paired with a true role model like Justin.

He brushed off the melodramatic description, and interjected with a calm smile, "Anything you can do to help us raise more funds would be deeply appreciated."

The KTLZ producer smiled back at him. "I'd be glad to help." She slid her cell phone into her pocket. "There's only one hitch. We would need to film ten days from now, and we want everything ready for the boys a couple of days before that."

Amanda did some quick calculations. "So we'd have a week." And she'd thought her agenda was impossible before!

"YOU SEEM TO be doing okay."

Justin looked up to see Amanda's grandfather framed in the office doorway. He stood to welcome A.B. "And

Amanda's not." Even though, for the past three days, he and Amanda had done nothing but work toward their respective goals. To the point where she had begged off spending time with him in the evenings and headed straight for her shower and bed.

Justin had let her go because he could see she was physically and emotionally exhausted, and he didn't want to deprive her of whatever personal space she needed. But there was no doubt he had missed their evenings together. Missed spending intimate time with her. Missed having the opportunity to make love to her again and solidify them as a couple.

A.B. took a seat in front of Justin's desk, his concern evident. "She has always worried she'll be rejected if everything is less than perfect."

That, Justin thought, was obvious. He went to the minifridge in the corner, got out two bottles of water, and handed one to his guest. "She didn't get that from you."

A.B. gave a long-suffering sigh. "Her parents required perfection of everything—and everyone—in their lives."

That couldn't have been a fun way to live. Justin took a long thirsty drink. "Does Amanda ever see them?"

"My wife and I arranged it, several times, after Amanda came to live with us, but her folks always came up with excuses and never showed up. Eventually, we just stopped trying to effect any kind of reconciliation. It seemed less hurtful."

Justin capped his bottle. "Where are they now?"

"Last I heard, her dad had married his fourth wife and was managing a big hotel on Maui," A.B. admitted. "Her mom—my daughter—is in California, weathering a sixth divorce."

"And you don't see them, either," Justin guessed.

"No."

Justin thought about how different that was from his own family, who, even when they disagreed with each other, still managed to work out their problems. "I'm sorry to hear that."

A.B. shook his head. "It is what it is. Wishing otherwise won't change that."

Justin rocked back in his chair, glad the older man had stopped by his office to chat before going to the bunkhouse to help Amanda and Lamar. "What will make Amanda feel better?"

"Zooming through the to-do lists. Achieving your goals. The big work party you've put together for tomorrow should go a long way toward accomplishing that."

Justin hoped so. Thanks to all the calls he'd made, they had plenty of people coming to assist. He had hoped Amanda would feel more confident as a result. She wasn't. Maybe because she hadn't ever seen what the people of Laramie County could do when they came together in a common cause.

Her grandfather obviously didn't share the same concerns. "You don't seem all that worried about her," Justin remarked.

"Normally, I would be." A.B. drained his bottle and screwed the cap back on. "Normally, this is the kind of situation that has her running as fast and far away as she can get. Instead—" the older gentleman smiled and inclined his head in the direction of the bunkhouse "—she's working harder and seems more committed to the cause than ever."

Justin knew that to be true. He smiled back. "We both are."

"Then take comfort in the fact that she's settling in instead of trying to move on." A.B. rose. "It's only when she has one foot out the door that you should start to worry."

BUT AMANDA DID have one foot out the door, Justin thought the following morning, as the board members and various friends and family—including his parents—arrived to help. It was evident in the fact she hadn't yet moved to her assigned quarters in the lodge, but insisted on staying in her trailer in the campground several miles away.

It was also evident in the way she managed to keep her physical and emotional distance from him while helping to organize and oversee the work.

By the time night fell, all the cabinetry had been finished, and three thousand square feet of unfinished wood flooring had been put in. The walls and trim were all painted. The entire crowd had been thanked and fed.

"We've made arrangements with a company in Dallas to provide the bunkhouse furniture," his mom had told him upon arrival.

His dad looked Justin in the eye. "I know there have been times in the past few months when your mother and I have both had our doubts, son, but that's over. Amanda helped us see how committed you are to the cause." Wade's voice caught. He gave Justin a hug, then pushed on, eyes glistening, "We're very proud of you, son."

It wasn't often his dad became emotional. Justin choked up, too. "Thank you both," he told his parents thickly as his mom hugged him, too. "This means a lot."

Meanwhile, nearby, Amanda's grandfather was deep in conversation with Miss Mim. Justin overheard her say, "Laramie Gardens is a wonderful senior-living village." Eventually, she convinced A.B. to give it a try.

"You're going to stay there tonight?" Amanda asked her granddad in disbelief.

"Laramie Gardens has rooms for prospective residents for a nominal fee. If I stay there, I'll be able to eat breakfast in the dining room and take the full tour tomorrow." A.B. seemed truly enthusiastic.

Amanda studied him in shock. "You would really consider leaving San Angelo and moving here?"

She didn't seem as happy to hear that as Justin would have expected, although she could just be attached to that home.

A.B. wrapped an affectionate arm around his granddaughter. "I want to be close to you, honey. And your future is here."

As the picnic dinner for all the helpers commenced, Libby remarked to Amanda, "Speaking of futures. When are you going to move into the lodge full-time?"

"Actually, I've been too busy trying to finish up the bunkhouse to think about it." Amanda stood up to get more iced tea. She brought the pitcher back to the folding banquet tables they had lined up across the yard. Then she made her way down the table, topping off glasses as she went.

Always thinking ahead, Mitzy added, "I think it should probably be done before the KTLZ crew arrives to film the segment on the ranch, don't you?"

Amanda smiled as if it were no big deal, when Justin knew that, to her, it was a very big deal. "I probably should."

"Do you want any help with that?" Justin's dad asked, misreading the reason behind Amanda's delay.

Justin jumped in, "We've got it covered, Dad."

At least, he hoped they did.

"So when did you want to move into the lodge?" Justin asked Amanda after all their guests had left. It was nearly midnight, and the two of them and the dogs were sitting, exhausted, on the front porch of the lodge enjoying the warm, starlit night.

Amanda brought her knees up to her chest and wrapped her arms around her legs. "I still have another four days."

Which meant she'd be waiting until the very last second before filming began, he realized. "We could do it tomorrow instead," Justin suggested mildly.

Amanda shook her head, stubborn as ever. "I want to stain the floors in the bunkhouse tomorrow, and when that dries put the first of three coats of sealant on."

Justin figured it would be unwise to push. She'd probably had enough of that at the dinner, anyway. He exhaled. "Okay."

She gave him a sidelong look. "You think I'm procrastinating."

Since she had opened the door to the next question, he returned her sidelong glance. "Are you?"

Amanda chewed on her lower lip. "Maybe."

His gaze traveled over her silky calves and bare arms. Reminded how beautiful her body was all over, he asked, "Any particular reason why?"

"One." She sighed wistfully. "You."

Was this going where he hoped it was? He sure as heck hoped his patience was about to be rewarded. His body hard and ready for action, he echoed softly, "Me." He needed and wanted her to spell out whatever she was thinking and feeling.

The corners of her lips turned up in a soft smile. "In case you hadn't noticed, it's difficult for the two of us to be alone together without making love. So, that being the case, maybe it would be best if we waited until the last minute for me to actually move in here. That way, when I do, we'll have a lot of built-in chaperones who can help us stay on the straight and narrow."

Knowing she needed a life of her own as much as he did, he pointed out casually, "Even after you move in, we'll still get time off to do whatever we please." Although they had to be mindful of their responsibilities, and the accompanying restrictions, working at the boys ranch didn't mean they forfeited a private life entirely.

She sighed wistfully, abruptly seeming miles away from him. "I know."

He waited until she met his eyes again, then said, "We'll still want each other."

She hesitated. "At least for a while."

Ah. So this was the real problem. One he could easily solve. "Not 'for a while,' Amanda," he corrected, taking her by the hand and drawing her to her feet. He slid his arms around her waist and brought her snug against him so she could feel how much he wanted—and needed—her to be his. He lifted a strand of hair from her cheek and tucked it behind her ear. "*Forever.* I'm not the kind of guy who changes my mind about that, Amanda. Once I commit to someone, I'm in it for the long haul."

The pulse in her neck was throbbing as she lifted her face to his. She gazed up at him, conceding softly, "And you're into me for the long haul."

He smiled and kissed her again, feeling victorious. "I'm talking absolute exclusivity."

Amanda wound her arms about his neck and kissed him back. "So," she said tenderly, "am I."

AMANDA HADN'T PLANNED to invite Justin back to her trailer that evening, but once he kissed her there was no going back. No pretending she wasn't falling head over heels in love with him. No pretending she wanted him anywhere other than with her, in her bed. That night, and every other.

They undressed the moment they entered her trailer and fell onto her bed, senses in an uproar. And from there it only got hotter as he drew her flush against him, letting her feel his hardness, kissing her without restraint.

Draping a leg over her legs, he continued caressing her breasts, ribs and thighs with his fingertips, before sliding lower to explore the most intimate part of her. And still he couldn't get enough of her, or she him. Desire exploded in liquid heat.

She arched blissfully, never more aware of the power one woman and one man could feel. Never wanting anything to endure more.

He moaned at the trail of kisses. "Amanda…"

"Let me love you."

He surrendered until he could bear it no more. Then rolled her over, captured her wrists and pinned them on either side of her head. Kisses followed. Slowly at first, then hotter, harder, deeper.

Amanda whimpered, opening her mouth to the pressure of his, stroking her tongue with his. She rocked against him, kissing him back, urging him on, until there was no doubt about what she wanted, what they both wanted. Tingly heat spread. Her feelings intensified as he slid his hands beneath her hips and lifted her to him. He entered with excruciating slowness, taking command in a proprietary way that electrified her.

Amanda cried out softly, pushing her fingers through his hair, smoothing her palms over his powerful shoulders and down his back, wanting him never, ever to stop.

And he didn't. Not until they both reveled in the erotic feelings, the sweet hot need, the sheer pleasure of being together. Pausing and withdrawing, going deeper every time until there was no controlling that, either. She was his…he was hers. For now, and forever.

Chapter Thirteen

Justin and Lamar were in the kitchen one morning later that week, wondering where Amanda was.

"It's nine-thirty," Lamar said. "Shouldn't she be here by now?"

Justin knew better than anyone just how early Amanda got up. This morning, they'd awakened at five o'clock and made the kind of love that just seemed to get better every time they were together. He'd left her heading for her tiny shower, come back to the ranch, taken care of the dogs and gotten a head start on his day.

Now, three hours later, still no Amanda.

"Should we go looking for her?" Lamar asked, his face pinched with worry.

"Go looking for whom?"

Justin and Lamar turned.

Amanda staggered toward them, buried under the weight of all she had slung over her shoulders and clasped in her arms.

Both guys quickly rushed to help. Justin took the heavy stand mixer with the stainless-steel mixing bowl and the cloth bag of perishable groceries. Lamar grabbed two big bags of assorted cooking utensils, gadgets and various baking sheets, which left Amanda with an oversize plastic clothes basket full of other food items and a cardboard box that had *food processor* scrawled across the side.

It looked, Justin noted joyfully, as if she was finally moving in.

"Why did you carry it all at once?" he asked.

"I didn't." Amanda announced cheerfully. She set the basket on the floor and unloaded her belongings onto the stainless-steel island in the center of the oversize kitchen. "There's more in my truck. So if you fellas are so inclined…"

Smiling, Justin and Lamar headed for the door.

"And don't forget the plants!" Amanda called after them.

Fifteen minutes later, they had unpacked everything. "What's this?" Lamar asked, holding up what looked like a three-foot wooden baseball bat that was narrower on each end. "Some kind of sports equipment?"

That would have been Justin's guess.

Amanda made a face. "No, silly. It's a French rolling pin."

"Ahh," both guys said at once.

Amanda took the pin and tapped Lamar playfully on his shoulder. "We're going to use it to make lunch today."

The teen quickly evidenced the panic Justin felt. What did either of them know about French pastry?

"What about the bunkhouse floor?" Lamar asked quickly.

"It only requires one more coat of sealant and that can't go on until about one o'clock this afternoon. We have to make sure the previous coat is really dry before we apply the last one."

Lamar's face fell, the way it always did when he had failed to get out of something he really wanted to avoid. "Oh."

Justin lifted his hands, already backing away. "Don't look at me. Much as I'd love to join you two chefs, I have to put the finishing touches on the big grant application for the Lone Star United Foundation. It has to be mailed today."

Amanda was glad she wasn't the one slaving over that huge stack of paperwork. "Well, good luck with that."

Grinning with relief, Justin disappeared.

Amanda turned back to her charge. Lamar was still looking at the long wooden rolling pin Amanda had inherited from her grandmother. He sighed. "I don't know about this…."

Amanda clapped a hand on his shoulder. "We had fun cooking before, didn't we?"

Another sigh. "Well, yeah, but…"

"And cooking is a skill you're going to need in life, isn't it?"

Lamar frowned. "I suppose."

"So I'm going to teach you how to use a recipe, because if you can follow instructions, you can cook practically anything with a little practice." She smiled. "And mark my words…you are going to be surprised at how easy it is to make pizza from scratch."

At the word *pizza,* his eyes lit up.

Giving him no more time to fret, Amanda dove in. She lined up the cup and spoon measures, brought out a packet of yeast, the flour, salt, sugar and thermometer.

Briefly, she went through what everything was, then handed him a glass cup. "This is a one-cup liquid measure," she said. "See how it's marked off?"

Lamar nodded, his expression serious.

"Run the tap water to warm, and then fill it to the red line on top."

He did as required, then brought it back to her. "Let's see how hot it is. We want it to be between 105 and 115 degrees." They put the thermometer in, waited. Amanda smiled as the thermometer registered 107 degrees. "Perfect! Now we open up the packet and take a teaspoon of yeast, sprinkle it over the water and stir to mix." She watched as he carefully complied, then gave him another reassuring glance. "Good. We'll set this aside and wait for the yeast to activate—which will take about ten minutes."

They went on to measure the flour, salt and sugar into the mixing bowl. Amanda showed Lamar how to check the yeast for bubbles, then slowly add olive oil, and the yeast-and-water mixture to the bowl. When it was all blended, Amanda sprinkled flour on the counter and dumped the dough onto it.

Justin walked in. He had a huge stack of papers. Amanda immediately recognized the big grant application. There were sticky notes protruding everywhere. "I've marked everywhere you have to sign and date," he said. "So if you want to do this now…"

Amanda looked at her hands, which were covered with flour. "Can it wait?"

Justin frowned, impatient in a way he usually wasn't. "This really needs to go out."

"If you put it on my desk, I'll get to it as soon as I'm done here."

He slid her a long look. "It has to be mailed today."

"I'm headed into town later to pick up the window blinds for the bunkhouse. I can do it then."

"By five?" he prodded.

Trying not to be annoyed by his unusually intense level of micromanagement, she nodded. "I promise. Okay?"

"I'll leave the mailing envelope and everything with it front and center on your desk."

"Thank you." Justin still seemed less than pleased by her response. Luckily, the tension was cut by the roar of what sounded like a tractor-trailer coming up the drive. She shot a look at Justin. "Are you expecting anyone?"

"Not today." Justin paced to the front door, looked outside and groaned.

Watching, Amanda called from the kitchen doorway. "What is it?"

Justin swore. "The bunkhouse furniture."

"JUSTIN SURE IS grouchy," Lamar noted several hours later.

"That's because it has been one of those days where everything that could go wrong has gone wrong," Amanda reassured him.

The bunkhouse furniture had been prematurely delivered, which meant it had to either be stored in the lodge or sent back to the Dallas warehouse and they'd have to wait another two weeks for redelivery. Sending the furniture back wasn't an option since the KLTZ crew was due to film their Local Heroes piece on Friday. While they were attempting to make room for the furniture, the state auditor had arrived to take a look at the ranch's books.

Justin had no sooner gotten the auditor situated in a room apart from his cluttered office than the architect had arrived—along with a surveyor—to decide the best place to situate the woodworking shop. The two men had driven in from Fort Worth and hadn't had time to stop for a meal en route. So Lamar and Amanda had ended up making more pizza and a huge salad, and inviting everyone— including the truck driver and his unloading partner—to stay for an impromptu lunch amid all the chaos.

"Everybody liked our pizza, though, didn't they?" Lamar remarked as they finished the last of the dishes.

Amanda smiled. Lamar was really getting the hang of thinking on his feet in stressful situations. "They really did." And with good reason. The meal had been excellent. No doubt about it. Lamar had an innate talent for cooking as well as carpentry.

"Are you going to teach all the kids that come here to cook?"

Amanda wiped down the kitchen counters. "I was thinking about it. What do you think?"

Lamar took care of the table. "They'd probably like it, too, although I don't know about all that recipe stuff."

She had noticed he'd seemed more confused than comforted by the written instructions. But then, she supposed that was normal for someone with zero experience in the kitchen. "You'll get the hang of it." Amanda paused to add a little water to the herb pots she'd situated along the windowsill.

"Maybe," Lamar looked doubtful. "But I like doing stuff that's easy to memorize."

Amanda walked outside with Lamar. They stopped at the shed to pick up the gear they needed before proceeding to the bunkhouse. "Are you ready to put the final coat of sealant on the floors?" Amanda checked to make sure all the windows were open, to ensure maximum ventilation and quicker drying time.

Nodding, Lamar picked up a can of polyurethane, a brush for the corners and tight areas, drip pan, and mop-style applicator. "You want to do it the same way we did it yesterday?"

"You start in the corner of each of the bedrooms, and work your way to the door. I'll do the kitchen and dining room and we'll meet up in the living room."

They worked well in tandem. By four o'clock they were outside, starting the cleanup, when her cell phone rang. Able to see from the caller ID that it was the chairwoman of the board of directors, Amanda stripped off her gloves and answered. "Hey, Libby. What's up?"

"Hi, Amanda. I was just talking with a friend of mine, who's overseeing the grant applications at the Lone Star

United Foundation. He said ours hadn't been received yet. I wanted to make sure it was in the mail, since it has to be postmarked today to be considered."

Oh, no. Amanda blew out a breath. "Justin finished it this morning." Somehow, she managed to sound a lot more with-it than she was. "I'm on my way to the post office right now." Or she would be, Amanda amended silently, as soon as she dashed inside the lodge to get it.

"Great," Libby enthused. "The post office in town closes promptly at five, you know."

Amanda tried not to panic. "Yes. Justin mentioned that." Her heart pounding, Amanda thanked Libby for the reminder and ended the call. She turned to Lamar. "I've got to go into town to mail something that's got to go out today. Will you be okay finishing the cleanup on your own?"

"Sure."

Amanda hesitated.

"I remember what we did yesterday," Lamar promised.

She knew he had an excellent memory. Far better than most kids his age. "Okay, but just to be sure…" She reached into her pocket for the small notepad and pen she habitually carried to mark down measurements. "I'm going to write out everything you need to do—in order. And don't forget, the rags and the used roller sponges should be left outside in the empty paint trays to dry. Everything else should be put in the shed with the door closed."

"No problem."

Amanda tore off the paper and handed it to him. Her pulse racing, she ran toward the lodge, dashed inside, slowing to a deceptively casual walk as she passed the room where Justin was hunched over a desk with the auditor, and then hurried into her office. She grabbed the huge stack of papers from the desk, a pen and the mailing envelope, then headed quickly back out again, aware she now had only forty-one minutes to get to the post office. And she hadn't even signed anything yet!

Racing against time, Amanda drove toward Laramie. Halfway there, she came across a small traffic jam, caused by a wide-bodied tractor mowing the berm. It cost her a good ten minutes. Shortly after that, several volunteer fire department vehicles, including a fire truck, passed her, sirens blazing.

Giving a silent prayer that whoever needed EMS was going to be okay, Amanda turned her attention back to driving and the directions on her dash-mounted GPS.

Unfortunately, she was so rattled she got turned around once she hit the historic downtown area, where she encountered another traffic jam caused by the usual early-evening rush.

Finally, she located the post office, a small square building with an empty flag pole in front of it, and no other cars in the lot. She parked her truck, just as her phone rang.

Justin.

Figuring it best not to talk with him until she had completed her mailing, she got out of the car and sprinted toward the door. And found, not surprisingly, that it was locked, since it was now 5:10. No reason to panic. She would just find another post office that stayed open later.

Amanda went back to her truck and consulted the internet via her phone. To her relief, she saw the main post office in the next county was open until seven. GPS directions estimated it to be about an hour away from her current location.

No problem. She would just go there.

Amanda started the ignition and headed out.

She was fifteen minutes outside the Laramie city limits when Justin called again. Figuring he probably wanted to know if she had indeed gotten the grant application mailed, she again decided not to pick up. Better to talk with him after she had completed the task as promised.

Unfortunately, he called her again two minutes later. And again, three minutes after that. Beginning to think something was wrong besides her bad memory, Amanda took the call. "Hey," she said, as if everything was fine with her.

Only to hear him sounding frantic on the other end.

"Amanda, thank God I reached you! I'm with Lamar at the Laramie Community Hospital E.R."

Her heart sank. "My God! What happened?"

"I'll explain when we see you," Justin promised in a low, clipped tone.

And Amanda knew, even without him saying, that whatever had happened was all her fault.

JUSTIN HAD NEVER been one to hover. He was hovering now, like the worst helicopter parent, and he didn't care. With the foster parents and Amanda still en route to the hospital, he was all the kid had. Justin was determined not to let him down.

Lamar teared up as he eased himself into a sitting position on the stretcher. His face smudged with soot, he looked incredibly young and vulnerable in the hospital gown. "Amanda's going to be mad at me."

Seeing Lamar so distraught made Justin want to lose it, too. He fought to remain as calm as the kid needed him to be. "No, she's not," he said soothingly. Glad a little dirt was all they worried about, he forced Lamar to lie back against the pillows. "And put your oxygen mask back on."

The exam room door swung open. Amanda rushed in. She was a mess. Justin had never been simultaneously so angry and so glad to see someone in his life. What had she been thinking, leaving Lamar to his own devices? Without even letting Justin know she was headed for town? Did she really think he cared more about the grant application than the teenager in their charge?

Oblivious to Justin's tumultuous emotions, she stared at Lamar, as if unable to take it all in, then rushed to hug the teen like he were her long-lost child. "Oh, Lamar!" She released him slowly and pivoted to Justin. *"What happened?"*

What happened, Justin seethed, was that Amanda had been incredibly irresponsible! Struggling with a burst of temper that he knew had as much to do with relief as it did anger, Justin snapped, "He put paint-thinner-soaked rags in the shed and shut the door. The combination of closed air and extreme summer heat caused them to ignite within, oh, say five minutes…."

Amanda clapped a hand over her mouth. More tears welled. "Oh, my God."

Lamar shook his head and started to cry in earnest, too. He shifted his mask again. "She told me not to do that, Justin. It's not her fault—it's mine. Look!" Coughing, he reached into his pocket and pulled out a crumpled paper as proof. "She wrote everything down for me."

Justin studied the familiar writing. Sure enough, the instructions she'd left were detailed and clear as day. *Air-dry the rags and paint rollers in the paint trays. Do not put in shed.* Beneath that, underlined, was, *Important—to prevent spontaneous combustion.*

"Why didn't you follow her instructions?" he asked Lamar, looking frustrated with both of them. "Especially if you had gone through this exact same procedure yesterday?"

Lamar looked even more frightened and on edge. "Because I…I…"

Sure the kid was hiding something, as well as doing all

he could to protect the woman he adored, Justin unleashed his anger on Amanda. "You realize we could be denied our license because of this?" If they weren't, it would be a damn miracle!

Amanda turned ashen. She looked confused, upset, humiliated, all of which made Justin feel worse.

"I—" Trembling, she choked back a sob. "I'm sorry." Trying to pull herself together, she finally looked from one to the other. "Is Lamar going to be all right?"

Thanking heaven for that, Justin nodded grimly.

Lamar nodded, too. "It's just smoke inhalation," he explained through his oxygen mask. "Because I smelled something burning and opened the shed...and...breathed in..."

Distraught, Amanda sank down into a chair. Completely overwhelmed, she buried her head in her hands.

Silence fell.

Justin stared at the crumpled notepaper, knowing instinctively there was more to this, something Lamar had yet to reveal. He turned to his young charge, wanting to help, knowing he would never be able to unless the teen was straight with him. "I know you have this thing about not following instructions," he drawled.

His efforts to prod the truth out of Lamar worked. The boy's jaw set. "It wasn't that."

"Then *what was it?*"

Lamar glared back at him. "You really want to know?"

Justin nodded and pushed even harder. "After what happened this afternoon, I think the least you owe us is an explanation!"

Tears sprang to Lamar's eyes. He threw up his arms, shouting belligerently, "I can't read, okay? I. Can't. Read. Anything! Got it?" Coughing, Lamar ripped off his mask and tried to swing his legs off the gurney.

Amanda leaped up, tears streaming down her face. She caught Lamar by the shoulders, just the way a loving mother would, and held him in place. She replaced his oxygen mask. "What do you mean, you can't read?" she asked gently, searching his eyes, sharing his pain.

Misery engulfed Lamar. "I just can't," he declared haltingly. "I never could."

"Which is why you hate school," Amanda said, with all the empathy a child could ever want or need. "Why you refuse to do your assignments. Why you skip class and didn't want to go back."

"Yes." Lamar broke down completely and thrust himself all the way into Amanda's arms. She held him tight. Eventually, Justin joined in. And that was the way the medical staff found them, clinging together, comforting, consoling, like the family they had become.

Chapter Fourteen

"Amanda knows we have a television crew coming first thing tomorrow to do the story on the ranch?" Libby asked at noon on Friday.

Justin looked at his longtime friend. "She's aware." *Very much aware, as a matter of fact.*

Libby watched him use a dolly to roll the last of the furniture down to the bunkhouse. Clearly frustrated with all the recent setbacks that threatened to derail the project they'd all worked so hard on, she asked, "Then, where is Amanda?"

Wasn't that the question of the day! Justin shrugged and headed back to the lodge to get the table lamps he'd already unpacked and assembled. "I don't know where she is. I haven't seen her since she left the hospital last night, after Lamar's foster parents showed up to take him home."

"Did she say where she was going?" Her low voice radiated with concern.

Justin exhaled. "She said something about finishing up a few errands, that she'd see me at some point after that."

"But Amanda didn't come back to the ranch last night."

"No," Justin replied tersely. "She didn't." Neither had she been at her trailer. He knew, because he'd gone back and forth between the two locations all night long and this morning, looking for any sign of her. There had been none.

Libby frowned. "Have you spoken to her grandfather?"

Justin nodded. "A.B. is in San Angelo. He said he hadn't seen her, either, but told me not to worry." *Like that was even possible.* "He thinks she'll show up eventually."

"I hope so." Libby checked her phone for messages. "Do you want me to call some of the other board members, help you finish setting up the bunkhouse?"

All Justin wanted at the moment was to be alone, to try to process everything that had happened. Irritated with himself for not having seen this coming, even though all the signs had been there, clear as day, he replied curtly, "I've got it. Thanks."

Libby touched his arm. Happily married herself, she wanted the same for him. Everyone on the board did. "Please call me if you need me."

He nodded, promising that he would.

After she left, Justin went back to carrying lamps. He was about ready to start setting up bunkhouse beds when the dogs jumped up and ran to the door. He walked outside and saw Amanda getting out of her truck.

She looked like she had showered and washed her hair since he had last seen her, but her face was pale and drawn, and she was wearing the same clothes she'd had on the day before. Where had she been?

She came toward him, an envelope in her hand. Her amber eyes glistened with a mixture of sorrow and regret, and suddenly he only wanted to know one thing. He caught her by the shoulders. "Are you okay?"

She nodded, then took a step back. "Can we talk?"

Aware they should have done this yesterday, before they left the hospital, Justin reached for her hand. She resisted his touch. Realizing she needed her physical space, he reluctantly drew away.

She crossed the yard to the lodge. Her shoulders taut,

she moved gracefully up the steps and sat down on the front porch.

The afternoon was blisteringly hot, but she did not appear to want to go inside the air-conditioned comfort of the lodge.

He followed her gaze to the burned-out shell of the shed.

Her lower lip trembled and tears filled her eyes. "It's ruined."

Justin settled opposite her. Still wishing she would let him hold her, he leaned against the rail, hands braced on either side of him. "Things can be replaced."

Amanda drew another breath, more shaky than before. "Sometimes they can," she agreed, sounding a bit stronger now. She paused, looking him right in the eye. "But sometimes mistakes can't be undone." Her jaw set. "I didn't get the grant application in on time yesterday." She tensed, forcing herself to go on, "The truth is, I got so busy I forgot all about it."

Justin had already ascertained as much. The application was the least of his worries when the woman he wanted more than anything seemed poised to storm out of his life as swiftly and unexpectedly as she had stormed in.

Amanda shook her head in mute regret. "The fact is, if Libby hadn't called me yesterday afternoon to inquire about it, I would have let the deadline come and go. But once she reminded me about it, I grabbed the grant application, left Lamar with instructions and ran off to the Laramie post office to mail it."

Justin could understand all that. He would have done the same thing. With one exception. "Why didn't you tell me where you were going?"

Her fingers tightened on the envelope in her lap. "Because I didn't want you to know I had come so close to failing the ranch." She scoffed in self-contempt, then continued softly. "I thought I could get there in time and make the deadline without you ever knowing I had screwed up."

Abruptly, Amanda got up, set the envelope aside and paced the length of the porch while Justin and the dogs watched in concern.

"But of course," she said, throwing up her hands, "the post office was closed by the time I got there." She finished recounting her story. "But, despite everything, I was determined to turn this debacle around. So after I left the hospital last night, I drove to Dallas, checked into a hotel and went to the Lone Star United Foundation offices first thing this morning to hand over the big grant application in person."

Impressed she had done all that instead of just throwing in the towel, Justin asked curiously, "Did they accept it?"

Amanda hung her head in shame. "No. Apparently, a deadline is a deadline. We're welcome to try again next year, of course, but that won't help us in the meantime… which is why," she went back to get her envelope and handed it over, "I'm resigning."

Justin took the letter only because he didn't want to tussle with her. Refusing to open it, he said, "You don't have to do that."

Amanda dug in her heels. "You spent weeks working on that grant application."

"There will be others." The stunning truth was, he meant it. He knew he could always find a way to fund-raise for the ranch. However, he couldn't replace the woman standing before him, the woman who had come to mean so much to him, the woman who had lit up his life like nothing that had ever come before.

"There shouldn't have to be other grants," Amanda lamented. She raked her hands through her butterscotch-blond hair. "The truth is, I never should have taken this job."

He set the envelope aside and stepped closer, still hoping to talk sense into her. He caught her by the shoulders again, holding her when she would have run. "Then why did you?" he asked quietly.

Tears spilled out of her eyes. "Because, Justin, I thought I could help kids who had been as unfortunate as I had been growing up. Make them feel cared for and valued, the way Granddad and Gran made me feel."

"Lamar felt—feels—that way, Amanda, and all because of you."

"And you."

An awkward silence fell.

"Face it, Justin, because I have. Lamar could have died because I didn't realize he couldn't read. When I think back on all the times I should have noticed…but I didn't even once suspect it!"

"You weren't alone in that."

She stepped closer, vibrating with emotion. "The point is, you didn't just accept his recalcitrance as par for the course the way I did. You asked the questions that led to his confession."

"It could just as easily have been you." And would have been, Justin knew, given a little more time.

Amanda sighed with palpable guilt and shook her head. "I don't think so." The dogs moved closer, trying to comfort her. She refused their loyalty and affection, too.

Once again, she turned her attention to the burned-out shed that was set to be removed in its entirety later in the day. "And let's not forget that I am the one who put Lamar in danger, too, by leaving him to finish up and clean those brushes alone."

Justin wasn't about to cast the first stone. "So you

learned a valuable lesson," he said, more than ready to forgive and forget.

She swung around to face him, planting her hands on her hips. "Like where I belong and where I don't."

Justin tried another way to reach her. "I understand what it is to fail a kid you want to help. To be so ticked off at yourself you want nothing more than to run away. I felt the same way when Billy Scalia died. But eventually I came to my senses, just as I am asking you to do now, and realized that blaming myself accomplished nothing."

"I disagree. It led you to move on, to where you belong, just as I intend to do."

That had an ominous ring. "You belong on this ranch, Amanda."

"No, I don't, Justin." More tears spilled. "I know what everyone thought, but they're wrong. I'm not a local hero. I'm not the role model the kids who come here are going to need. You are."

Her declaration hit him like a sledgehammer to the chest. And suddenly, Justin knew. "You were never going to stay, were you? Never going to leave behind your no-madic ways and move into the lodge for good." He regarded her with deep disappointment. "You were always going to leave." He had just been too foolishly hung up on her to see the truth. "It was just a matter of when." Bitterly, he walked away from her.

She followed, hands outstretched, wanting his forgiveness if nothing else. "That's not true," she protested.

"Isn't it? This whole time you've had one foot out the door. It's why you're rushing to get out now."

Silence fell. She wanted to deny it. In the end, he noted sadly, she couldn't.

"We can still see each other—from time to time."

Her offer was a pale imitation of what they could have

had. He shook his head, his mood every bit as melancholy as hers. "No, Amanda, we can't do things halfway. You're either in this all the way, or you're out."

"You don't mean that."

The hell he didn't.

He set his jaw. "If you walk out on this ranch now, it's the same as walking out on me." The one thing he wouldn't—couldn't—tolerate was another woman who put her own needs or wants above their relationship.

"Then I'm out," Amanda said sadly, her heart every bit as trampled as his. "Don't you see?" She covered her eyes and walked away. "I have no choice."

ONE WEEK LATER, Amanda sat in front of the television in her granddad's home, watching—and rewatching—the KTLZ segment on the soon-to-open Laramie Boys Ranch.

There was no doubt about it—Justin was amazing. Everything the kids would need in a mentor. Plus, incredibly well-suited to run the ranch. The board members were also interviewed in the segment, but it was Justin's vision, drive and energy that stole the day.

And had stolen her heart.

Amanda sighed. If only she hadn't let him down. Let everyone down. But she had, and there was no going back. No use in her ineptitude dragging everyone else down.

The doorbell rang. Irritated—because the last thing she felt like was talking to anyone—Amanda paused the recording and went to answer.

Libby, Miss Mim and Mitzy stood on the front porch. "A.B. said we would find you here," Libby said.

Amanda wasn't surprised they'd had no trouble tracking her down. A.B. had been spending a lot of time in Laramie courting Miss Mim. Whereas Amanda had needed time alone. Out of politeness, she ushered them into her grand-dad's small, neat, one-story home.

She shut the door behind them, and mindful of Miss Mim's age, guided them into the sitting area so the older woman could sit comfortably. "If you're here to dress me down for botching up the big grant application, there's no need. I take full responsibility for not getting it in on time, and I feel absolutely terrible."

"It's not an apology we need," Mitzy said, taking a seat on the sofa, looking as much social worker as friend.

Libby sank into an armchair with her usual elegance. Miss Mim took the other. All noticed the freeze-frame of Justin and the boys ranch on the TV screen.

Amanda flushed and hastily switched it off before sitting beside Miss Mim on the sofa.

All eyes swung back to her. "We're here because we need you to come back, Amanda," Libby said.

Mitzy added, "Justin and Lamar most of all."

The notion that she might be missed as much as she missed the two of them hit Amanda square in the heart.

She swallowed. "I'm sure my leaving left a temporary gap in how things were running," she acknowledged reluctantly. For one thing, she had been doing most of the meal planning and cooking. "But I assure you, Justin is more than capable of picking up the slack."

Attempting to ease the tension in the room, she shook her head ruefully and said, "Just don't hire him to do any carpentry. That is definitely not in his skill set. The same way administrative duties are not in mine." He was better at rescuing homeless dogs and kids, and even women—like her—who had never experienced true, romantic love....

Libby sobered. "We realize now that we threw too much at you at once and have accepted your resignation in the spirit in which it was given. Justin has been appointed ranch director."

Something was finally as it should be. "That's good news," Amanda said with relief. At least she hadn't messed that up for Justin. Especially since he had more than deserved to have the job all along. She leaned forward. "How is Lamar doing?" She knew he had completely recovered from smoke inhalation, but other than that...

"Justin arranged to have Lamar tested last week, and we discovered he has dyslexia."

Amanda paused to absorb that. "So, since no one helped him with his disability, he's had great difficulty learning to read."

Mitzy nodded. "Now that we understand what the problem is, we can bring special teachers to the ranch to help him instead of putting Lamar back into the high school, where he could not possibly succeed at this time."

No wonder he hadn't wanted to sign up for classes at LHS. Amanda felt a twinge of guilt for having forced the issue without delving more deeply into the real reason behind Lamar's truancy.

"At Justin's urging, we've also decided to focus on students with learning disorders such as dyslexia or dysgraphia," Libby said happily. "Grouping them together that way will help the kids realize they are not alone."

"That certainly makes the selection process easier," Amanda said.

Miss Mim sighed. "Sadly, there are far too many kids who need this kind of help. Which is why we want to continue our efforts to quickly expand the funding and the facilities at the boys ranch. And we need your help to do that. Both as the head of the carpentry vocational program and as assistant ranch director."

Amanda wanted to help, more than they knew. She had

only been there a month, but the ranch still felt like home to her in a way no other place ever had. Which, maybe, was what scared her. The idea that she would come to rely on being there, only to be booted out, the way she had been by her oft-divorcing parents when she was a kid.

Nevertheless, even though she was tempted to jump at the chance to go back, she felt obligated to remind them, "I not only failed in my previous employment there, but failed badly." To the point she'd had no choice but to quit in disgrace, lest she drag Justin—and the ranch—down with her.

Kindness radiated from her visitors.

"We all make mistakes," Mitzy said. "What's important is showing the kids that when you fall down, you pick yourself up, dust yourself off and keep going."

"What's that saying? 'You learn more from any failure than you ever do from any success,'" Libby quoted from memory.

Miss Mim leaned over and patted Amanda's hand. "Lamar is counting on you to help him through the tough months ahead, to provide the emotional support and understanding only you can give. You can't let him down."

Suddenly, Amanda was near tears. But she blinked them back, refusing to let herself hope until she knew. "What does Justin think about this?" she asked.

The three ladies knew the answer to her question. That was clear from the way they looked at each other as they stood and prepared to leave.

Miss Mim regarded her with a poker face. "That, you will have to ask Justin yourself."

"Got a minute?"

Justin turned to see A. B. Johnson framed in the door of his office. For a brief moment, he hoped that Amanda had come with her grandfather, but A.B. was alone. Justin rose and the two men shook hands. "What can I do for you?" he asked cordially.

"You can hear an old man out."

Appreciating A.B.'s efforts to do right by his beloved granddaughter, Justin gestured for the older gentleman to have a seat and waited.

A.B. cleared his throat. "Years ago, when Amanda's parents started having problems, I did my best to stay out of it. In retrospect, I wish I had interfered. Because if I had sat them both down and talked to them about the importance of taking the time to work things out, instead of just getting divorced, maybe everything would have turned out differently."

Justin paused. "You think her parents are still in love with each other?"

A.B. shook his head. "I think they never had a chance to find out what true, lasting love is, because they didn't hang in there long enough to find out. Instead, they became fixated on the infatuation stage of a relationship, where everything is easy and great, and never learned what it is to work through your problems with the person you love, difficult as that may sometimes be."

Justin wished it were that simple. "That's not the case with Amanda and me."

The older man watched him skeptically. "You're saying you were never infatuated with each other?"

Justin scoffed. "We were plenty attracted." To the point he figured he would never get over her.

A.B. pressed on, "You were never friends, then."

Justin wished everyone weren't so interested in sizing up his emotional state—and offering ways to fix his problems with Amanda. "Amanda and I had the potential to be great friends."

"But anything permanent wasn't in the cards for you."

Justin made no effort to hide his growing frustration. "We never got that far." Although there had been a brief time when he'd dreamed of just that.

"Exactly my point." A.B. smiled.

"I appreciate you stopping by and trying to help…" Justin rose to his feet.

A.B. remained seated. "But?"

Justin sighed and sat back down again. "All my life I was taught that I could achieve anything I set my mind to, if I just wanted it bad enough. And worked hard enough." He swallowed around the clenched feeling in his throat. "I thought the same thing applied to my relationship with Amanda."

A.B. nodded compassionately. "Until she quit her job here and took off."

Exactly. "I can't make her want to be here. That has to come from inside." He pointed to the center of his chest, wishing he did have Amanda's heart. "And I sure as heck am not going to be with someone who doesn't value our relationship above all else." He had done that before. He wasn't doing it again.

"I see your point."

"You just don't approve."

A.B. stood up and moved slowly toward the door. "I think you're taking an easy out."

Justin stopped Amanda's granddad before he could leave. "In what way?"

Their eyes met, man to man. "In accepting her declaration that everything—her relationship with you, her taking a job here, even her getting involved and mentoring Lamar—was all a terrible mistake."

He *had* tried to talk sense into her! Only to have her head for the hills, anyway. "What would you have me do?" Justin lamented.

A.B. clapped a paternal hand on Justin's shoulder. "Fight for her as hard as you fought for this ranch. Let her know that you accept there will be setbacks and you're okay with that." He paused. "Because what you *will* have together, if you both take that big leap of faith, will surely be worth it."

JUSTIN THOUGHT ABOUT everything Amanda's grandfather had said, and he was still thinking about it when he went out to take care of the new ranch sign. He parked beneath the archway over the entrance, grabbed his toolbox and hopped up into the bed of his truck.

He was just trying to figure out how to unfasten the wooden Lost Pines Ranch sign from the metal arch when a familiar red truck pulled up behind him.

Amanda got out, her straw hat with the sassy rolled brim pulled low over the sunglasses shading her eyes. Wearing the same short denim skirt, layered tank tops and flip-flops she'd had on the first time they'd met, she sashayed toward him. "Hey there, fella," she said.

He tried not to get too excited as he surveyed every gorgeous inch of her. "Hey there, yourself," he returned softly, getting down from the bed of the truck. Did her sudden appearance mean what he hoped?

She studied the lopsided sign above them, shook her head and heaved a dramatic sigh. "I heard you were going to attempt this yourself," she drawled.

"I can handle it."

Amanda strode toward him, her beautiful blond hair glinting in the sunshine. As she neared, he couldn't help but inhale the citrus scent of her perfume.

"I'm sure you can." Amanda stepped closer to inspect the rusty screws bolting the weathered wood to the old iron frame. She took off her sunglasses and hooked them in the neckline of her tank top. "The thing is, you shouldn't have to." A pulse worked in her neck as she swept off her hat and set it aside. "At times like this," she declared, "a man needs a partner." Her voice caught and she pushed on hoarsely. "The kind of mate who can be counted on to be there through thick and thin." She paused again, moisture glinting in her pretty amber eyes. "The kind of partner my gran and granddad had in each other."

Now they were getting somewhere. Justin fitted his hands around her waist and brought her even closer. "You're talking marriage?"

For the first time since she had arrived, she hesitated. "Longevity."

He chuckled. "What's the difference?"

She tipped her head up. "I don't know," she challenged. "You tell me."

He wanted her, but needed a real future with her and hoped that she realized that, too. "Longevity could just mean living a long time," he pointed out.

She splayed both hands affectionately against his chest. "Nothing wrong with that."

Justin threaded his hands through her hair and searched her face, still hardly able to believe she was here. Softly, he warned, "I'm not going to be content with an affair, even a long-term one. I want rock-solid commitment. Marriage." *With you, damn it all.*

His throat closing, his voice rusty, he pushed on. "I want to be with someone who isn't afraid to commit to me and our union for the rest of her life. Someone who wants to work by my side during the day and sleep in my arms at night. Someone who is ready and willing to take care of this ranch and all the kids who come to it…and maybe even have a baby or two of our own with me."

Her eyes glistened with heartfelt emotion. "That's a tall order," she allowed finally.

He gave in to the desire assailing him, lifted her face up and brushed his lips across the softness of hers. "Made for a tall woman."

She moaned with a mixture of humor and pent-up passion. "Are you making fun of my height?"

Knowing no other woman had ever made him this happy, or ever would, he shook his head. He kissed the top of her head. "Your height is one of the things I love best about you."

She let out a contented mewl and curled against him. "You know, if we did ever have kids they'd likely end up being seven feet tall."

He stroked his hand through her hair. He had missed her so much. "Then I guess we'd be looking up at them."

"We might have to raise a ceiling or two."

"Or just build the ceilings extra tall to begin with," he joked.

Amanda drew a breath and stepped back, as if needing distance to say what she had to. She flashed a wobbly yet sincere smile. "Before we get too sidetracked…the way you and I always tend to do…I want you to know something." She paused, her gaze roving his face as if memorizing it for all time. "I came here, first and foremost, to apologize with all my heart."

"For?"

She met his level look. "Walking out on you and letting you and the ranch and everyone associated with it down."

He would have forgiven her for that, even without the formal mea culpa. He nodded, hoping this wasn't the beginning of another kiss-off. "Apology accepted."

Amanda knitted her hands together. "I also came here hoping you'd take me back."

Personally? Professionally? Her wary expression gave

no clue. "As assistant director?" He tried to keep the question offhand.

Amanda nodded confirmation. She rushed on while his heart was still turning over in his chest. "And girlfriend, and friend, and potential life mate or wife. However you want to say it." She lifted a staying palm. "I don't care. I just want to know that we can start over."

He liked the sound of that. Justin tugged her against him, chest to chest, thigh to thigh. He buried his face in the fragrant silk of her hair. "Or pick up where we left off."

Amanda clung to him, all artifice gone. She kissed him breathlessly. "And know that we'll be here for each other, through all the ups and downs of life."

What do you know? That was exactly what he wanted. Justin smiled. "I think we can handle that." They indulged in a leisurely kiss. "You know why?"

Her eyes were misty with happiness as she shook her head.

"Because we're meant to be together." Knowing it was time to let the rest of the barriers go, he regarded her seriously and confessed all he'd held back. "And because I love you, Amanda, and always will."

Amanda went up on tiptoe and kissed him. Hotly. Eagerly. "Oh, Justin," she whispered, trembling all the more, "I love you, too, so very much."

He pressed his lips to her temple, aware he had everything he had ever wanted, at long last. "So, it's a deal?"

Amanda looked deep into his eyes. "Absolutely, we have a deal! I'm yours. And you're mine. From here on out…"

Epilogue

Fifteen months later...

"Do you want to choose what's for dinner, or shall I?" Amanda asked her husband as they walked into the kitchen of the cozy cottage built just for them.

Justin met her at the refrigerator to survey the contents. "Depends on what we've got planned for later," he teased, appreciating—as did she—the intimacy their new living arrangement offered.

Amanda slid her arms around his neck. "Same thing as always, I expect." She nestled closer.

Justin grinned and bent his head to demonstrate. "A little kissing."

Amanda tenderly kissed him back. "A lot of cuddling."

They sighed in unison. "And everything in between."

They made out a little more, then, still tingling with anticipation, Amanda shook her head. "I can't believe it's December of our second school year already!"

Justin shook his head in wonder. "Or that you and I've been married nearly six months." He paused, reflecting. "The past sixteen months have been quite a ride, haven't they?"

Yes, they had, from the very beginning. The boys ranch had opened a year ago August, right on schedule, with

Lamar, seven other boys and two house parents settling into Bunkhouse One. Amanda, Justin and a teacher specializing in learning disorders had bunked in the lodge.

The carpentry building had been completed in late fall of the initial term. And by spring they'd had the funds to add another bunkhouse, eight more kids, another set of house parents and two more full-time teachers. Now, they were planning a third bunkhouse.

"Your granddad has had a lot of great changes, too." A.B. had sold his business and his home in San Angelo, and relocated to a condo in the Laramie Gardens senior-living center.

Amanda smiled. "Can you believe he and Miss Mim are getting married on New Year's Eve?"

Justin sat down on a chair and pulled her down onto his lap. "I knew something was up when they both started volunteering at the ranch so much." Granddad had helped out, teaching carpentry to the boys. Miss Mim had set up a ranch library, complete with Dewey decimal system and online catalogue.

"And let's not forget Lamar." Amanda's heart brimmed with affection. "Not only has he learned to read, he's become quite the leader."

Justin agreed with paternal pride. "There's no one better when it comes to showing the new kids the ropes."

Amanda splayed her hands across his chest. "It helps a lot, having specialized teachers and a curriculum designed specifically for dyslexics."

In fact, they had been so successful the county was talking about starting up a day program for kids with learning disabilities from stable homes, to be paid for by the school district and held in classrooms out at the ranch.

Reveling in the warmth and strength of her handsome

husband, Amanda continued, "It also helps to have such a visionary at the helm of the entire ranch."

Justin stroked a hand through her hair. "And his trusty assistant director and carpentry and culinary whiz…"

They kissed again, even more tenderly. She'd always known she loved working with her hands. Helping kids. But… "I never thought I'd enjoy being a sidekick quite so much." She chuckled as they broke apart. "But maybe that's because you do all the paperwork."

Justin's eyes gleamed with satisfaction. "We do make a good team."

"One," Amanda added mysteriously, her heart beginning to race with excitement, "that may be ready for expansion."

Justin studied her as the wonder of her words sunk in. "You're…?"

"Almost three months along," she admitted, thrilling at the contentment in his blue eyes. "I found out when I went to the doctor today. I wanted to wait until we were alone to tell you."

Justin threw back his head and laughed in triumph. He brought her close for another heartfelt hug. "This is glorious news, Mrs. McCabe."

Amanda couldn't stop smiling. "I think so, too."

Happiness engulfed them as their fondest dreams began to take shape. "So what do you think?" Justin brushed the hair from her face and tucked it behind her ear. "Girl or boy?"

Amanda rested a palm on the gentle slope of her tummy. "I don't know about this one," she enthused with a playful wink. "But I imagine before we're done we'll have both a son and a daughter." At least she hoped.

Justin thought of his own family. "Or five sons."

Not to be outdone, Amanda exclaimed, "Or five daughters!"

They stared at each other and laughed. All Amanda knew for sure was that the ranch was a roaring success. She was going to have Justin's baby. And she had never been happier.

Justin shifted her off his lap, swung her up in his arms and strode toward the rear of the house. "Where are we going?"

"Exactly where you think." He paused and kissed her, the love flowing freely between them. "To celebrate."

* * * * *

Watch for the next installment in the
McCABE HOMECOMING *miniseries,*
THE TEXAS CHRISTMAS GIFT,
coming December 2013, only from
Harlequin American Romance!

REQUEST YOUR FREE BOOKS!
2 FREE NOVELS PLUS 2 FREE GIFTS!

HARLEQUIN

American ★ Romance®

LOVE, HOME & HAPPINESS

YES! Please send me 2 FREE Harlequin® American Romance® novels and my 2 FREE gifts (gifts are worth about $10). After receiving them, if I don't wish to receive any more books, I can return the shipping statement marked "cancel." If I don't cancel, I will receive 4 brand-new novels every month and be billed just $4.74 per book in the U.S. or $5.24 per book in Canada. That's a savings of at least 14% off the cover price! It's quite a bargain! Shipping and handling is just 50¢ per book in the U.S. and 75¢ per book in Canada.* I understand that accepting the 2 free books and gifts places me under no obligation to buy anything. I can always return a shipment and cancel at any time. Even if I never buy another book, the two free books and gifts are mine to keep forever.

154/354 HDN F4YN

Name _____ (PLEASE PRINT) _____

Address _____ Apt. #

City _____ State/Prov. _____ Zip/Postal Code

Signature (if under 18, a parent or guardian must sign)

Mail to the **Harlequin® Reader Service:**
IN U.S.A.: P.O. Box 1867, Buffalo, NY 14240-1867
IN CANADA: P.O. Box 609, Fort Erie, Ontario L2A 5X3

Want to try two free books from another line?
Call 1-800-873-8635 or visit www.ReaderService.com.

* Terms and prices subject to change without notice. Prices do not include applicable taxes. Sales tax applicable in N.Y. Canadian residents will be charged applicable taxes. Offer not valid in Quebec. This offer is limited to one order per household. Not valid for current subscribers to Harlequin American Romance books. All orders subject to credit approval. Credit or debit balances in a customer's account(s) may be offset by any other outstanding balance owed by or to the customer. Please allow 4 to 6 weeks for delivery. Offer available while quantities last.

Your Privacy—The Harlequin® Reader Service is committed to protecting your privacy. Our Privacy Policy is available online at www.ReaderService.com or upon request from the Harlequin Reader Service.

We make a portion of our mailing list available to reputable third parties that offer products we believe may interest you. If you prefer that we not exchange your name with third parties, or if you wish to clarify or modify your communication preferences, please visit us at www.ReaderService.com/consumerchoice or write to us at Harlequin Reader Service Preference Service, P.O. Box 9062, Buffalo, NY 14269. Include your complete name and address.

HARI3R

SPECIAL EXCERPT FROM

H HARLEQUIN®

American Romance®

Check out this excerpt from
CALLAHAN COWBOY TRIPLETS
by Tina Leonard,
coming September 2013.

Tighe, the wildest of the Callahan brothers, is determined to have his eight seconds of glory in the bull-riding ring—but gorgeous River Martin throws off his game!

Tighe Callahan sized up the enormous spotted bull. "Hello, Firefreak," he said. "You may have bested my twin, Dante, but I aim to ride you until you're soft as glove leather. Gonna retire you to the kiddie rides."

The legendary rank bull snorted a heavy breath his way, daring him.

"You're crazy, Tighe," his brother Jace said. "I'm telling you, that one wants to kill you."

"Feeling's mutual." Tighe grinned and knocked on the wall of the pen that held the bull. "If Dante stayed on him for five seconds, I ought to at least go ten."

Jace looked at Tighe doubtfully. "Sure. You can do it. Whatever." He glanced around. "I think I'll go get some popcorn and find a pretty girl to share it with. You and Fire-freak just go ahead and chat about life. May be a one-sided conversation, but those are your favorite, anyway."

Jace wandered off. Tighe studied the bull, who never broke eye contact with him, his gaze wise with the scores of cowboys whom he'd mercilessly tossed, earning himself a legendary status.

"Hi, Tighe," River Martin said, and Tighe felt his heart start to palpitate. Here was his dream, his unattainable brunette princess—smiling at him as sweet as cherry wine. "We heard you're going to ride a bull tomorrow, so the girls and I decided to come out and watch."

This wasn't good. A man didn't need his concentration wrecked by a gorgeous female—nor did he want said gorgeous, unattainable female to see him get squashed by a few tons of angry luggage with horns.

But River was smiling at him with her teasing eyes, so all Tighe could say was, "Nice of you ladies to come out."

River said, "Good luck," and Tighe shivered, because he did believe in magic and luck and everything spiritual. And any superstitious man knew it was taunting the devil himself to wish a man good luck when the challenge he faced in the ring was nothing compared to the real challenge: forcing himself to look into a woman's sexy gaze and not drown.

He was drowning, and he had been for oh, so long.

*Look for CALLAHAN COWBOY TRIPLETS
by Tina Leonard, coming September 2013, only from
Harlequin® American Romance®.*

SADDLE UP AND READ 'EM!

Looking for another great Western read? Check out these September reads from HOME & FAMILY category!

CALLAHAN COWBOY TRIPLETS by Tina Leonard
Callahan Cowboys
Harlequin American Romance

HAVING THE COWBOY'S BABY by Trish Milburn
Blue Falls, Texas
Harlequin American Romance

HOME TO WYOMING by Rebecca Winters
Daddy Dude Ranch
Harlequin American Romance

*Look for these great Western reads and more
available wherever books are sold or visit*
www.Harlequin.com/Westerns